DANGEROUS REVENGE

A LUCA MYSTERY
BOOK 11

DAN PETROSINI

Print ISBN: 978-1-960286-11-6
Naples, FL
Library of Congress Control Number: 2023901537

ACKNOWLEDGMENTS

Special thanks to Julie, Stephanie and Jennifer for their love and support, and thanks to Squad Sergeant Craig Perrilli for his counsel on the real world of law enforcement. He helps me keep it real.

OTHER BOOKS BY DAN

1

A CHARCOAL GRAY CLOUD FORMATION HAD SNUFFED THE light out of the sky. I checked my watch. It was 2 p.m. A gravel path led to a trailer tucked in the woods off Santa Barbara Boulevard. We were a mile off Davis Boulevard, and somehow the property hadn't been developed. Yet.

Derrick had a contact we hoped would help us cripple a drug ring that had moved in. I knew it was important work, but it just didn't cut it for me. Homicides were my thing. Being a narc wasn't.

Without a murder to solve, I dug into cold homicide cases. Most detectives liked active investigations, but not me, especially a drug case. My distaste for them was compounded by a lack of experience.

Derrick caught me looking at my watch and said, "What time was her appointment?"

"One." Mary Ann had gone to the neurologist. She said it was routine, but I'd noticed she was tiring quickly, and it concerned the hell out of me.

"Every doctor's office is jammed up these days."

"Probably." I pulled out my phone. No text. "All right, let's get this over with."

The walkway to the pale blue trailer was lined with a rusty bike and more tires than a gas station.

"I hope this guy gives us something."

"Making us come all the way out here, he better."

Derrick knocked on the door. My phone rang. It was Mary Ann. Derrick knocked again and I stepped away. "What did the doctor say?"

Mary Ann was telling me about a new prescription as Derrick disappeared into the trailer. Shots rang out. I shoved my phone in a pocket, drew my weapon, and screamed, "Derrick! Talk to me."

No reply. My back pressed against the trailer, I cracked open the door with the nose of my pistol. My lunch backed up into my mouth. A pool of blood was forming near Derrick's neck.

"You all right?"

Derrick mumbled, and I heard what sounded like someone jumping to the ground. I ran around the side of the trailer. A six-foot male in a black hoodie was running away.

My vision tunneled. I dropped to a knee. Aiming, I pulled the trigger.

I heard my gun cycling but the shots themselves were muffled. The suspect stumbled and I fired again. He began to fall and I shot again. And again.

I ran up to him and put two more bullets into his back. I nudged him with the toe of my shoe. He was dead.

My hearing returned. Digging my phone out, I ran to the trailer. "This is Detective Frank Luca. We have an officer down. Nine-nine-nine. Officer down. Get a medic unit rolling. Now!"

I gave our coordinates and knelt by my partner.

"Hang in there, buddy. Help is on the way."

Blood seeped out of a wound where his shoulder and neck met. Derrick tried to speak.

"Don't talk. Save your strength, man." Tears rolled down my face. I took my vest off and tore my shirt up. I put the cloth on the wound and applied pressure. Blood soaked through. I pressed harder.

"Don't close your eyes, buddy. Look at me. You're going to be okay. Come on, man, don't go to sleep."

As the sounds of sirens drew near, I caressed his cheek. It was cold. "Hang in there. They're coming. You hear the sirens?"

His eyes closed as the medics burst in. "Hurry! He was hit in the neck area."

The medics put an oxygen mask on Derrick and wrapped a pressure dressing around his neck. On the phone with a doctor, I heard the medic say Derrick's pulse was weak, had lost a lot of blood, and they suspected he had a collapsed lung.

I sat on the floor trying to replay what had happened. How had I let him go in alone? Why did I go after the ambusher? I should have let the killer go and called for help as soon as I saw Derrick was shot. Every second counted with a gunshot wound. I'd let my partner down.

Derrick was lifted onto a gurney as two uniformed officers came in. Ignoring the question of what went down, I followed the stretcher out as a crime scene van and police vehicles pulled up.

I wanted to ride along, but the details of the tragedy needed explaining, and I wanted to examine every inch of this hellhole. They closed the doors to the ambulance, and, saying a prayer, I noticed someone approaching.

Detective Lacey was a no-nonsense kind of guy. He'd

been on the streets for two decades and was considered a good cop before going inside. However, eight years as the director of internal affairs made him less sympathetic to the dangers and split-second decisions officers had to make.

Without extending a hand, he asked what had happened. I gave him a quick rundown of what had transpired, and he said, "We're going to need your weapon."

It was standard procedure. I handed it over. Bagging it, Lacey said, "Where is the alleged shooter?"

Alleged? "This way."

"Put booties on and watch where you step."

Circling away from the path used by the shooter, we came to the body. Lying on his right shoulder, he was crumpled into a semi-fetal position. Lacey surveyed the area then bent over the corpse. He stood, exchanging glances with the uniforms.

"Where were you when you fired?"

I pointed behind me. "A couple of paces off the trailer's corner."

"Did you announce your presence, asking him to halt?"

Everything happened so fast, I hadn't. "He knew I was here."

"Is that a yes?"

I couldn't admit I shot first. "Yes."

"And he kept fleeing?"

"Yes."

"Did he threaten you or point a weapon in your direction?"

"He shot my goddamn partner, for Christ's sake."

"I'm aware of that, Detective Luca. What I'm trying to understand is why you fired six shots into his back."

"Don't you even try to turn this shit around on me. This sleazebag ambushed Derrick. You want to talk to me, do it downtown. I have a crime scene to process."

"You're prohibited from participating in this."

I turned around. "My partner was shot!"

"That doesn't matter."

I gave him the finger and walked to the trailer. My mind was hopping from Derrick's condition, to why this had happened, to indignation over Lacey's insinuation.

2

___

Pulling on gloves, I stepped into the trailer and was hit with the smell of mildew. Two walls were streaked with black mold. It felt like it was the first time I'd been inside. The filth of the place came into focus. In a snapshot, I realized no one had lived there in years.

Footprints of blood led to a pool of it on the right, where Derrick had fallen. To the left was a kitchen area, anchored by an aluminum card table. Sitting on the old table was a broken scale used by drug dealers to weigh their poison.

Rags, empty bottles, and aging fast-food wrappers were strewn on the floor. By the toe plate under the sink lay a glassine envelope. It had a pair of capital *C*'s on it. What was the meaning of that? Were these drug dealers so brazen they created a logo for their crap?

A stained mattress and old magazines were all that was in the bedroom. The window was open. It was the one the shooter left through. I stuck my head out. Lacey stood by as the corpse was placed into a body bag.

The dead guy was surrounded by a police contingent.

Who was with Derrick? How would his wife, Lynn, react? I had to get to the hospital.

I poked my head in the bathroom. The sink hung off the wall and the shower stall had no door. Why was this place chosen for a meetup if the ambush wasn't planned? I went outside and pulled my phone out to call Mary Ann.

"Derrick's been shot."

"Oh my God. How is he?"

"It's bad. Took a bullet to the neck area just above the neckline of the vest. He's on the way to Physicians Regional."

"Is he going to be okay?"

"He better be. Look, get over to Lynn's and tell her what happened. If she doesn't have anyone to take care of Wendy, then take the kids with you and get to the hospital. I'll meet you there. They need us."

DERRICK WAS IN SURGERY. The waiting room was a sea of beige uniforms. I'd already lost one partner. It was from a heart attack, but he had been my best friend. My brothers kept coming up to me, but I was in no mood to talk to anyone. I went outside to wait for the girls.

Mary Ann and Lynn ran toward the entrance. I met them halfway and wrapped my arms around them.

Lynn had tears in her eyes. "How is Derrick?"

"He's in surgery."

"Tell me, is he going to make it?"

I had my doubts but not about sharing them. "Of course, he will."

"Thank God. If I lost him, I don't know what we'd do."

"Let's go in."

"What happened? Tell me."

I told them what had happened, leaving out several details as Sheriff Chester pulled up. We quickly exchanged greetings and headed into the hospital.

THREE HOURS LATER, Lynn was told the doctor wanted to speak to her. I took Lynn's hand, escorting her down a hall. A doctor in blue scrubs was toying with his phone. He pocketed the device when I cleared my throat.

The physician smiled thinly, extending his hand. "Mrs. Dickson, Dr. Blaine. Your husband is out of surgery—"

"How is he?"

"He's critical but stable. The bullet did substantial damage in the thoracic region and ricocheted into an upper vertebra. Your husband has lost a lot of blood and has a collapsed lung as well."

Lynn wobbled. I put my arm around her waist. "Is he going, going to be okay?"

"It's early, but we believe he'll recover."

"Oh, thank you."

"There may be some struggles along the way—"

Instead of telling him to shut his damn mouth, I said, "Can she see him?"

"Yes, but only for a moment. He needs to rest. Follow me."

Beds lined both sides of the recovery room. We went toward a bed where a pair of nurses hovered over Derrick. He had a tube down his throat and a spaghetti bowl of lines and hoses leading to bags on poles. Lynn's knees buckled, and I struggled to swallow as I caught her.

She sobbed while patting Derrick's arm. I had to look

away, staring at a squiggly lined monitor as she reassured Derrick he'd be all right. As we were asked to leave, I silently vowed to get everyone and anyone responsible for the assault.

Handing Lynn off to Mary Ann, I went to brief the sheriff on Derrick's condition. Chester shook his head.

"His poor wife, with a newborn, no less. I'm going to see if there's anything we can do for the family. Look, you need to get back and make a statement."

Nodding, I let the girls know I'd be back as soon as possible and headed for the exit. I stopped short. On the other side of the glass doors was a group of reporters and a cameraman. They were like sharks who'd smelled blood.

Backing up, I scooted out a rear exit used by ambulances. Walking to my car, I was enveloped with a surreal feeling. This nightmare was snowballing. Having internal affairs conduct a colonoscopy on me was expected, but I hadn't considered the press.

I climbed into the Cherokee and sat there. How the hell did this happen? What could I have done to prevent my partner from lying in an ICU room?

As the senior member of our team, I was responsible for him and, de facto, his family. I pushed Lynn's terror-filled face from my mind and started the car.

As I drove, I went over my story. The reality was that until Lacey said I had shot him six times, I hadn't given it a thought. It was a foregone conclusion that IA was going to claim it was excessive force. To an outsider it'd appear so, but not in the instinctual mode I had been in.

My responses had to be truthful but couched in a certain way or I'd find myself in deeper trouble. There'd be an investigation into every aspect of my actions. I understood it and backed a reasonable assessment anytime an officer fired his gun.

It was serious business, but this was different. We were ambushed. Unfortunately, I knew that wouldn't mean much to IA, especially when deadly force was deployed.

I was less concerned about being charged with murder, though it was a possibility. The fact the victim was a gang member who'd shot an officer would be hard to ignore, no matter how righteously it was framed by those with low opinions of law enforcement.

It was so obvious. They shot first. Derrick was lying in a hospital fighting for his life. How could they think otherwise? They'd see the light. The thing to worry about was the health of my partner. He was in a bad way.

What the hell had I'd done? If I would have stayed with Derrick, he'd have a better chance of recovering, and I wouldn't have to defend my actions. Why hadn't I? Now I was stuck defending myself.

I'd probably be forced to sit behind a desk until a complete airing of the incident was finished. Or would it be something worse? Either way, I wouldn't be able to track down who was responsible for setting the trap Derrick walked into.

3

———

The conference room in internal affairs was freezing. Lacey had his sports jacket on. I didn't know if he was projecting formality or trying to keep warm.

Lacey didn't ask a single question as I explained what happened at the trailer. When I finished, he said, "Why was Detective Dickson alone in the trailer?"

"I was right behind him, but something caught my attention, so I stood outside for a moment."

"What was it?"

"Before I could check it out, I heard the gunshot."

"You fired six shots at the gunman. All entering his back. Was he a threat?"

"He shot Derrick, for God's sake. Of course he was a threat."

"He was running away."

"He was armed. I had no idea what he would do next."

"His weapon was found tucked into the front of his pants."

"It was my judgment at that time to ensure he was

neutralized. It's my duty to eliminate any threat to public safety."

"That's all for now, Mr. Luca."

Mister? Had the decision been made to suspend me rather than some kind of administrative leave? If that was what was coming, I had little time to figure out who the hell was behind the ambush.

I ran down the stairs to my office and searched the property records for the owner of the trailer. The tax assessor's office listed Ray McKinley as the owner of the land. There were no improvements listed on the bill. The county didn't seem to know a trailer was parked on it.

Nothing came up on McKinley besides a twenty-four-year-old speeding ticket. He didn't have a current driver's license. I went into the DMV portal, discovering that he failed to renew his license in 2017. That was probably because he was now eighty-six years old.

Though the chances were slim that McKinley was connected, I owed it to Derrick to check him out. I took a picture of the address with my phone and took the stairs back up.

Collier County didn't have a dedicated narcotics detail, which was why I'd been asked to work this case in the first place. It's not that Naples was insulated from the scourge of drug use. We had our share of users, but the problems they created were far different than those of a large city.

Instead of dealing with strung-out addicts mugging old ladies to feed their habit, we had people wrapping their German autos around light poles and a cell full of people drying out.

Most of the people in town abusing prescriptions or using illicit drugs had the money to fund their addiction. In fact, it was probably the money that got many of them into trouble in the first place.

Sergeant Cisco ran the general crimes unit and was the drug expert by default. Six foot three, and measured, he was one of the handful of people actually born and raised in Naples.

"How's Derrick doing?"

"He took a hollow point to the neck area. He's in ICU."

"Jesus Christ. I heard you put six shots into the bastard."

Word spread fast, especially in institutional settings. "It was surreal, you know."

"They didn't put you on admin leave?"

"Not yet. Since I'm the only able-bodied homicide dick, I'm hoping I can stay on, even if it's just behind a desk."

"Good luck with that. I heard the county is putting out a reward for information."

"Let's hope it helps get the bastards."

"What about IA? They putting you through the wringer?"

"Asking questions at this point." I lowered my voice. "But you know how Lacey enjoys crawling up your butt."

"Tell me about it. We have three separate investigations going against my guys."

"Good luck."

"We're gonna take up a collection for Derrick's wife, to help as best we can."

"That's nice; she'll appreciate it."

"It's the least we can do."

"Take a look at this. See if it means anything to you." I pulled up a picture of the glassine envelope found in the trailer. "It looks like a logo or something."

"It seems familiar. The drug cartels are branding their products like they're a legit business. Hold on a second, and I'll check with the DEA."

Driving to see McKinley, I rolled around the idea that a Mexican drug cartel was trying to extend its reach into Collier County.

The closest cities the cartels had a known presence in were Miami and Daytona Beach. Was the envelope evidence that one of them had decided Southwest Florida was an attractive market? Or was it just some user taking his poison in the trailer, who panicked?

The idea a frightened user shot Derrick faded as I drove east on Immokalee Road. At this time of night the notoriously busy road was empty, and I breezed along, turning into Huntington Lakes.

McKinley lived in one of the brown buildings lining Marsh Creek Lane. His unit was on the first floor of a multi-family structure. The only light visible was coming from the TV. I rang the bell, slamming the door with the heel of my hand for good measure.

A woman with an accent I recognized as Filipino opened the door.

"Detective Luca with the Collier County Sheriff's Office. I'd like to speak with Mr. Ray McKinley."

"Mr. McKinley?"

"Yes."

"Uhm. He's not able to talk much."

"Is he here?"

"Yes."

"I'd like to see him."

"Is this about his son?"

"No."

"Come in."

She flicked on the lights as we walked into the family room. McKinley was sound asleep in a reclined wheelchair.

"Wake him up, please."

She shook his shoulder, repeatedly calling his name. It took almost a minute for McKinley to open his eyes.

"This is a policeman. He wants to talk to you."

"Mr. McKinley, you own a piece of land on Santa Barbara Boulevard. Who do you rent it to?"

The reply was mumbled. The only word I caught was mother.

"He gets very confused. It's the dementia."

"Who takes care of his affairs?"

"His son used to, but he passed away a year ago. Now his daughter does. She's in Indiana."

"I'd like her contact details."

She wrote down a name and number.

As she showed me to the door, I asked, "How long has he been like this?"

"Mr. McKinley wasn't bad before his son died. Then he really slid."

"Terrible losing a child."

She nodded. "Especially when it's from an overdose."

"His son died from drugs?"

"Yeah, so sad."

"When was that?"

"A year ago."

It felt there was a connection.

4

I circled the kitchen telling Mary Ann the latest on Derrick's condition. When I punched a number into my cell, Mary Ann said, "Who do you keep calling at this hour?"

"The daughter of the guy who owns the land the trailer is sitting on."

"She probably shut her phone off. It's after midnight. I'm exhausted. I'm going to bed; you coming?"

I grabbed the car keys off the counter. "I can't go to sleep with Derrick lying in the hospital."

"There's nothing you can do. The doctors are taking care of him."

"That's bullshit. I can let him know I'm there for him."

"You're really going to the hospital?"

"Yeah, I can't sit around here."

"You need to sleep. You're not going to be helping anyone if you don't get some rest."

I felt like crap. My body was crying for a break, but my mind was crying for action. "I'll lie on the couch, and see if I can catch a couple of hours."

"Come to bed, Frank. I don't want to sleep alone on a night like this."

She was right. I was exhausted and followed her into the bedroom. As Mary Ann washed up, I called the hospital. There was no change. Derrick was still critical.

We slipped between the covers and she grabbed my hand. "He's going to be all right."

"I hope so. He lost a lot of blood."

"They gave him a couple of pints. He's where he needs to be."

"They say they don't know if the damage to his spine is going to be permanent or not."

"They can fix almost anything these days."

"I feel so bad for Lynn."

"Me too, but you know she's stronger than you think."

Most spouses of cops were. They had no choice. Anytime your partner went to work, there'd be a nagging worry until they returned. You were never prepared for something like this, but the reality was it wasn't a total surprise.

"She's staying with him, right?"

"Her mother lives in Cape Coral; she had to go pick her up to watch the baby."

I sat up. "He's going to be alone?"

"Derrick's not alone. There's a lot of people taking care of him. Don't worry, before you know it, he'll be back on the job."

After what happened to him, it wasn't clear he'd go back to law enforcement, regardless of whether he recovered or not. It made me ponder if I wanted to do this anymore.

His shooting and the threat of something happening to me hadn't sunk in yet, but I could sense a change in outlook that was being kept below the surface by adrenaline and confusion.

"I don't care if he ever walks a beat again as long as he's all right."

"Absolutely." She turned on her side and kissed my cheek. "Let's get some sleep."

The words just tumbled out of my mouth. "I took a life today."

"You did what you were trained to do."

"I don't know. I may have gone a little overboard."

She grabbed my hand. "You were ambushed."

"The guy was taking off. I shot him in the back."

"He was armed, right?"

"Yeah, but—"

"There's no buts. He shot one of us and was fleeing. Who knows who he would have fired on next? You probably saved a life or two."

She was making me out to be a hero of some kind. I knew I wasn't. "I should've called for help first, but I went after him."

"You had to make a split-second decision. Don't start doubting yourself. You eliminated the threat. I would've probably done the same thing."

Probably? "I don't know."

"You're going to be put on leave, you know."

"Maybe there's a way for me to stay active. That way I can help find who the hell was behind this."

"I wouldn't count on it."

"We'll see."

"Let's go to sleep."

She turned over, and within a minute her breathing slowed. How did she fall asleep so quickly? On a normal day it was tough for me, but tonight, every time I shut my eyes, I saw Derrick bleeding on the trailer's floor.

I replayed the episode for the hundredth time, and the

reality that I'd killed someone hit me. There was no doubt he deserved it, but I debated whether I should have shot to incapacitate rather than to kill.

It was an emotional reaction. Understandable in most people but not acceptable in my line of work.

I slid out of bed and went into the closet to get dressed. Mary Ann wouldn't be happy, but she'd know I was at the hospital. My holster was hanging on the belt rack. I slipped it on and opened the gun safe.

The pistol I used to kill had been turned in. I reached for my black Glock and hesitated. I thought about leaving without a firearm, but I hadn't been unarmed in two decades. Much as I didn't want to touch a gun, I forced myself to pick it up.

I GOT out of the Cherokee. It was warm, and the tropical wind messed with my hair. I breezed past a lone reporter, who was stopped from following me by a uniformed officer, and went into Physicians Regional.

You'd never know it was the middle of the night by the activity in the intensive care unit. I nodded at an officer sitting outside my partner's room. Hesitating, I entered.

My bladder cancer had required opening my abdomen and creating a bladder out of my intestines. It was a rough surgery, but on my worst days I never looked as bad as Derrick did. I kept swallowing at the thought of having a tube shoved down my throat.

I stroked his hand. It was cold. A nurse came in. She smiled and fiddled with one of the lines feeding into Derrick. I said, "How's he doing? He's going to be all right, won't he?"

"You'll have to ask the doctor. I really don't know much. My job is monitoring the IV bags."

"But you think he's going to be okay, don't you?"

"I'm sure he will. But it's best to ask the doctors." Before she finished speaking, a machine began beeping. She checked the monitor, took Derrick's pulse, and ran out of the room.

I was trying to assess whether Derrick's face was getting paler when two men and a woman in lab coats rushed in. One asked me to leave.

"What's going on?"

"Sir, leave the room. Now!"

I stepped outside as two aides bolted in. I went to the nurses' station to find out what was happening when Derrick was wheeled out of his room. Stepping toward my partner, a nurse corralled me. "He's going into surgery. He may be bleeding internally."

Blood pounded in my ears. Shaking my head to clear my vision, I asked God to save him and went into the bathroom. After splashing water on my face, I called his wife and the station.

Alone, I sat in a room for families. Why had I wasted time and chased down the killer instead of tending to Derrick first? He was up, almost able to talk. I thought there was time. I tried to calculate how much time I spent going after the shooter. Why didn't I call for help as I chased him?

It probably was no more than two minutes, three max. It didn't seem like much, but I knew it was more than enough to bridge the gap between life and death. I tried to assess what Derrick would have done if the situation were reversed.

Would it matter? Could Derrick ever forgive me? Could I forgive myself?

5

———————

I WAS IN A FOG. MY SIDE WAS KILLING ME FROM THE WAY I had fallen asleep, and my phone was ringing. It took me a while to get out of the chair. My legs felt like concrete. For some reason, I answered the phone.

"Hello?"

"Is this Detective Luca?"

"Yeah, who is it?"

"Diane McKinley. You called me a couple of times."

It was the daughter of the man who owned the land the trailer sat on. "Hang on a second."

I left the family room and leaned against a wall. "Thanks for calling back. Your father owns a piece a property where a police officer was shot."

"Oh, my God."

"I understand your brother died of an overdose."

"Yes, he did, over a year ago. What does that have to do with anything?"

"How long was he using drugs?"

She exhaled. "Since his early twenties. He didn't get into the hard stuff till he was about thirty, and then it got out of control. He went into rehab a couple of times, but he couldn't, he just couldn't stay clean."

"Do you know who he bought his drugs from?"

"I have no idea."

"What about some of his friends, people he used drugs with?"

"This guy, Peter Gist, he's the one who got him started."

She didn't know where to find him, but we'd track him down. The question was whether that was the connection that led to the trailer on her father's property.

A nurse told me that Derrick was in recovery. The surgery had gone well, but he was critical. I needed coffee before I could face Lynn. Walking to the cafeteria, the sheriff called.

"How is Detective Dickson?"

"He's out of surgery. It seems to have gone well, but he's critical."

"I'm praying for him."

"We all are."

"You know there's going to be a thorough investigation of this."

"I understand, sir, but it was unavoidable."

"IA will judge the appropriateness of the actions taken."

"But we were ambushed, sir."

"That may be the case, but my hands are tied. We have to let the investigation play out."

"But can't you intervene on my behalf?"

"There's no buts. The very nature of internal affairs is to provide an impartial, independent assessment of a situation. I can't be seen as interfering."

"It was unavoidable, sir."

"Department protocol is to put you on administrative leave—"

"I have to be able to hunt down whoever did this."

"I don't know if there's even a way we can bring you inside."

I was going to be sitting behind a desk in a best-case scenario. "Am I going to be suspended?"

He hesitated. "Why don't we let the investigation progress?"

"How much time do I have?"

"Almost none."

The sheriff had shown his colors. Again. He was putting distance between us. Chester always played it safe, like a politician. I understood it, to a degree. But where were the private words of assurance, support?

I HAD TO SLEEP. Driving home, I was in a weird state. My mind was racing, but my eyelids were heavy. Stopped at the Fifth Avenue and Tamiami Trail intersection, a stream of people crossed the street.

They were going about their day, shopping, eating, and sightseeing without a care in the world. Yet I was weighed down by a partner fighting for his life, my guilt over how it happened, and the growing worry that I'd be suspended and unable to arrest whoever was responsible for the ambush. Added to all that—I'd killed someone.

I bounced between attempting to sort out the crazy cocktail of emotions I was experiencing, to trying to suppress the depressing reality. It was playing mental tennis with myself, and I was losing.

Between anger, overwhelming sadness, and exhaustion, I couldn't think straight. Derrick had to get better, and I had to get justice for him and get internal affairs off my back. Then and only then could I evaluate whether it was time to find a new career.

I started thinking of easy-peasy jobs, like renting beach chairs or starting a home-watch service. My pension would cover most of the bills; I'd find something. Then I thought of Jessie going to college. I'd signed up for the Florida State program, so as long as she went to a state college, her education was covered.

It would work out, I thought, until Mary Ann's MS crashed the party. Who knew what kinds of changes and expenses would head our way if her condition worsened? It may have been extreme fatigue or frustration, but I couldn't see myself in law enforcement any longer.

IT SOUNDED LIKE JESSIE. It took my eyes a couple of seconds to focus. It was two o'clock in the afternoon. It felt like rubber bands were holding me down. Dragging myself out of bed, the reality that Derrick was in the hospital and that I'd killed a man rushed back.

I collapsed onto the bed and pulled the sheet over my head. How was I going to get past all this? My phone was vibrating on the nightstand. I reached out and grabbed it. It was Dr. Bilotti. I let it go to voice mail.

Couldn't I just lie in bed for a couple of months and get up when this nightmare ended? As long as Derrick was going to be okay, that was all that mattered. If the department wouldn't back me, screw them.

They could kick me off the damn force if they wanted. Being a cop had lost its appeal. I had a wife with MS and a daughter to think about and couldn't run the risk of getting killed. Let them catch the bastards who shot Derrick.

Without me, they had no homicide department. If Derrick

miraculously recovered overnight, he wouldn't be able to hunt for those responsible for shooting him. As the victim, he had to stay clear of the investigation. With Derrick sidelined and me retired, or suspended, there would be no one to get justice.

It took years to train someone to hunt killers. By then, whoever was behind the conspiracy to ambush Derrick would be long gone. It was up to me. But was I up to it? There was only one way to be a cop; you had to be in it a thousand percent. If you weren't, your odds of getting hurt or killed multiplied exponentially.

6

———

I STAYED IN BED UNTIL I HEARD MARY ANN AND JESSIE IN the pool. It took Mary Ann about forty-five minutes to swim her laps. Her twice-a-day routine helped in her battle with MS. The aerobic exercise had increased her strength and balance and decreased her spasticity.

It was time to get out of bed. I threw on shorts and a T-shirt and put a pod in the coffee machine. My girls were in the middle of their carefree day while I was besieged with worry.

Splashing milk into a cup, my cell rang. It was Dr. Bilotti. Again. He was a good medical examiner and a better friend. I wanted to swipe it away but answered.

"Hello."

"Frank, are you all right? I called five times."

"Sorry, Derrick went back into surgery and—"

"I know. I've been checking on him regularly. He's stable at the moment."

"That's better than critical, right?"

"Not exactly. It's a term we use to express no change in a patient's condition."

"You can tell me, Doc. Is he going to be okay?"

"From what I'm told, he's in a tough fight, but he'll pull through."

Pulling through and a return to normalcy were worlds apart. "He better do more than pull through."

"I'm sure he will. How are you doing? You on leave?"

"Not officially. This whole thing is a frigging nightmare."

"One day at a time. Derrick will be okay."

"That's all I want, Doc. He gets better, I don't care what Chester and the IA bastards have to say. I'll leave the damn force before they bounce me off."

"Take it easy. You're not going anywhere. Look, I wanted you to know we finally got an ID on the body. The border patrol had a record on the victim. They caught him crossing the border four times. His name is Gustavo Flores, a Salvadoran."

"So it wasn't the informant we were going to meet."

"No, and Flores looks to be a member of the MS-13 gang."

"MS-13 in Collier County?"

"It may be. He had their telltale tattoos."

"They're as violent as you can get. They'll shoot you if you walk on the wrong street in El Salvador. He deserves to be dead."

"You shot him six times."

"Yeah?"

"The second one ripped open his aorta, killing him instantly."

"So what? How would I know that?"

Bilotti hesitated. "You have to be prepared to be questioned over this."

"They're already busting my balls. They should be thanking me instead."

"They're going to look at the fact that all the bullets entered the back of the victim."

"He was running, I couldn't let him get away after shooting Derrick."

"Two of the bullets were shot at close range."

"What is that supposed to mean?"

"I'm not judging anything, Frank. I trust you and the split-second decisions you were forced to make. I'm trying to tell you that the autopsy is going to detail the number and location of each bullet wound, including the lethal one. It won't be highlighted, but the fact that two rounds were fired at close range will be in the report."

"There's nothing I can do about that."

"That's true, to a degree. I think you should give some thought to how you're going to respond to the inquiry. Have you considered having an attorney?"

"A mouthpiece? That'll make it seem like I have something to hide."

"It's the right thing to do. Between what happened to Derrick and IA asking questions, you're going to be under tremendous pressure. A lawyer can help you deal with the process. They'll make sure nobody says anything that makes things worse and be an advocate for you."

"I have to think about it. The union rep left a couple of messages. I'm sure it's what he wanted to talk about."

"It's the right thing to do."

"The right thing is to let me catch the bastards who did this. They started it."

"You're going to have to leave that to somebody else."

"Yeah? Who is that going to be?"

"The sheriff will deal with that."

"Maybe I should quit and go after them as a private citizen."

"I think it'd be a good idea for you to take a step back at this point. Take care of yourself. You've been through a traumatic experience."

"I'm fine."

"You may not realize it, but what happened is going to take a toll on you. I've seen it before, and you have too."

He was right. Two New York City cops I'd gone to John Jay College with slid downhill after getting rolled over by the department. One had shot dead an eight-year-old boy who wouldn't heed his command to disarm. The kid was hard of hearing and the pistol wasn't loaded. How he was considered wrong was the worst of the social justice movement.

"I'm okay."

"This is not the time to play macho man, Frank."

"I know."

"There's no shame in talking to someone about all this."

"The department is going to make me talk to their shrink. Chester makes anyone who fires a weapon go."

"It's a thoughtful approach."

On paper it was. Despite privacy laws, people talked. The problem was if anyone spilled their guts to the department's psychiatrist, they were as good as gone. I understood it to a degree. If someone was really in a haunted state, they shouldn't be patrolling the streets. But on the other hand, the point was to talk things over and reframe whatever had happened.

I didn't have the patience or the time to deal with the political end of things. It was better to quit. Retiring was growing more palatable. I tried to recall the end-of-year statement the department sent me.

To get a full pension, I needed just shy of two years more service. But I was somewhere near 85 percent, which seemed like more than enough at this moment.

7

―――――

THE SHERIFF WANTED TO SEE ME, AND I KNEW IT WAS ABOUT sidelining me. I sat in my chair, staring at Derrick's desk for a long minute before looking at my emails. I went over the previous day's arrests. Nothing stood out.

There were scores of messages from the men and women of the department offering their support. It was a community I was proud to be part of but would soon be separated from. An email with "Final Notice" in the title caught my attention.

I had avoided requalifying as a marksman, using the time to spend with Mary Ann. Now I only had fifteen days left. If I didn't qualify before I was put on leave or suspended, I might not be able to get certified.

That was one problem I didn't need piled on. I had ninety minutes before I had to see Chester, more than enough time to visit the basement range.

Only one of the eight lanes were occupied. We chin nodded to each other, and I adjusted my ear protection. The first target I clipped onto the line was a male full-body silhouette. I gave a thumbs-up to the technician in the booth. He sent the cardboard outline to the fifteen-yard marker. It was considered close range, and you were expected to be near perfect.

At the academy, my marksmanship trainer considered twelve to fifteen yards the magic distance. He continually stressed that we should strive to keep that distance from a suspect. He said it gave you time to assess a subject and their behavior while affording you a high-hit ratio if you needed to fire.

I filled the pistol's clip and slammed it into the grip. As a check, I grabbed the gun with both hands and, aiming at the target, checked its sights. Closing my left eye, I felt my hands tremor slightly and was hit with the smell of mildew. Something wasn't right.

The last time I fired, I'd killed a man. I couldn't shift from life and death to shooting practice rounds. If I tried to qualify now, I'd fail.

I took a couple of deep breaths and picked up the phone to communicate with the tech. "Hey, Barney, I haven't fired this one in ages. I'm gonna run a clip before we start."

"No problem, Frank. Let me know when you're ready."

I wrapped both hands around the handle and quickly squeezed off a shot. It missed the target completely. Shaking my head, I took more time. I centered the sight on the silhouette's chest and, holding my breath, fired. The bullet pierced a shoulder. I was off by ten inches. Oh for two.

It was time to change it up. Bringing the target in, I holstered the pistol and dropped my hands. I drew and fired with one hand from my hip. A belly shot. Reholstering, I pulled the gun out and fired again. A neck hit. For some reason, my hip shots were always good. I was thankful the first part of the test was the holstered hip shot.

Running the target back to the fifteen-yard mark, every one of the six shots hit. But I was taking too much time calming myself down before each shot. Accuracy was a big part of passing, but the time element was just as important.

Half the tests required shots being fired with a maximum of two seconds between rounds. One, the two-handed position, required firing twelve shots within forty-five seconds, including reloading your gun. If my hands shook, I'd flub the reload.

I filled the cartridge and fired eight consecutive rounds. Five hits. I needed 80 percent of forty-two shots to hit the targeted areas or I'd fail. Counting the hip shots as golden, I'd need twenty-eight of the remaining thirty-six to succeed.

Signaling my readiness, I reeled in the target and affixed a new one. As the tech sent it out three yards, I reloaded and holstered. I took a breath and hit the timer. I drew and shot from my hip. Bang, bang, bang, bang. Four for four. I exhaled.

The next part was also close range but from a two-handed high-point stance with a ready gun. The hard part about this was the time element—two shots in a second. If you failed this part you didn't deserve to own a gun. I went six for six and only needed twenty of the thirty remaining shots to hit.

They moved the target to the seven-yard mark. I only hit nine of twelve. My cushion slimmed to eleven of eighteen. Still a good margin, but the remaining shots were at the farthest distance, the fifteen yards I screwed up earlier.

The last two stages were two-hand high points drawn from the holster. The first was all about time – twelve rounds in forty-five seconds with a reload. I reeled in the target and put a new one on. As the tech sent it out, I assured myself everything was good.

The clock began its countdown. I put my hand on the gun's grip. As one melted to zero, I drew and emptied my pistol. Ejecting the cartridge, I put in another one, raised the gun, and fired four more shots. Putting the firearm down, I squinted. How many had scored hits?

There were only six good ones. I told myself it was the hardest part of the test but that meant I had to go five for six on the next stage. I changed targets and reloaded.

The light went from red to green, and I drew, bringing my hands together. I held my breath and squeezed the trigger six times before breathing. I scanned the target, three body hits and one head shot. Two were inches above the right shoulder, but one by the neck looked marginal.

I needed it to pass. Reeling in the target, I fist pumped. It breached the outline: I'd passed. It was a relief but also the worst performance of my career.

CHESTER WAS WEARING a red tie and a funeral face.

"Sit down, Frank."

"Thank you, sir."

"How is Detective Dickson?"

"Derrick's doing better. He's in serious condition but out of ICU."

"Good. I'll be going to see him later today."

"He appreciates the support, sir."

"His wife said they don't need anything, but do you know otherwise?"

"They're making the best of it. Right now, they seem okay. When he gets home, it might be a different story."

"Please keep an eye on it. You see something the department can do, bring it to me immediately. It's the least we can do."

"I'll do that, sir."

He picked up a document. "A couple from Port Royal put up a hundred thousand dollars to add to the reward."

"That was nice of them."

"Indeed. I'll bet there'll be more to come. Now, how are you doing?"

"Me? I'm fine."

"I think it's best for everyone if you took a little time off."

"I can't do that, sir. Not with everything going on. I need to catch who was behind this."

"I understand your desire for justice, but rules are rules."

"You're putting me on administrative leave?"

"I'm afraid so."

"Oh, come on, sir. Can't I just get desk duty? I can help there."

"I understand your disappointment, but I can't make an exception, especially at this point in the investigation."

8

————

Back in my office, I had half a mind to take my personal items with me. There was a chance I was never coming back. If they didn't force me out, I might be ready to pack it in. Let them see how they do without me.

Chester had floated the idea of bringing a detective in from Lee County, believing the threat would pressure the department into getting a solve. It was a ridiculous supposition.

It wasn't a mark against the fellow officers in Lee. The fact was, just getting up to speed in another department pulled your productivity down. Calling in outside reinforcements during a manhunt was something I supported, but a temporary reassignment of a detective who had a full caseload in another county smacked of desperation.

Grabbing my favorite picture of Jessie off the credenza, I headed out. Before closing the door, I took a look at Derrick's empty desk and decided to go to the hospital instead of home. About to enter the parking lot, I heard, "Hey Frank! Hold on."

It was Tim O'Leary, a lab technician. "What's up?"

"Sergeant Cisco said you were interested in the residue found in the envelope from the Dickson incident."

"That was no incident, it was a damn ambush."

"Uh, sorry, I mean, yes, the ambush."

"What did you find?"

"It was a combination of a majority of cocaine and heroin with some fentanyl. The street name for this is Joy Ride. There was a DEA bulletin a while ago on this mixture. It's a highly addictive concoction and can be deadly."

"Has the lab seen this brew in the county before?"

"No. It's a first for us."

<hr>

I EMBRACED LYNN. "How's he doing?"

"Better, he's been up most of the day."

"Hey, buddy, how are you?"

Derrick smiled.

"Man, you look great. How are you feeling?"

He whispered something unintelligible. I put my ear close to his lips. "What's that?"

"What happened?"

"We were ambushed."

He tried to pick his head off the pillow, and Lynn said, "Rest, Derrick. There'll be plenty of time to talk about what happened. You need to get strong."

Derrick whispered again. I couldn't hear it, but I read his lips. He wanted to know what had happened. I pulled a chair over and leaned in.

"We were meeting an informant at a trailer sitting off Santa Barbara Boulevard. You entered and got hit. I got the bastard. He jumped out of a window and I nailed him."

Derrick closed his eyes and shook his head ever so

slightly. I said, "They put me on leave, but I'll get every last one of them. Don't you worry. Nobody screws with my partner."

Derrick opened his eyes and smiled. He tried to talk, but I said, "Listen to me, what you need to do right now is get better. I've got the rest of it under control. You rest and get ready to come back to work because I'm not doing your job forever, you know."

He smiled again and nodded. I had to go see the department's shrink and was grateful that an aide came in to take Derrick for a test. Seeing him interacting a little gave me a high I'd need to sustain me through the appointment.

GARY ROSEN WORKED out of an office in the Collier County Health Department. It was across the street from the sheriff's offices. I parked behind the building and took the stairs to the third floor.

The difference from Dr. Bruno's setting was depressing. Even factoring that I wasn't there voluntarily, the place felt forced and industrial. It was all about utility. In comparison, Bruno's office was in a home that smelled like someone was baking. It was there to put patients at ease, and it worked.

Rosen was pudgy, with thinning auburn hair and John Lennon glasses. "Mr. Luca, it's nice to meet you."

"Hello, Doc."

We settled into two chairs, better suited for a waiting room, around a glass table.

"I've read a summary of what occurred. I'd like to ask you a couple of questions."

"Go ahead."

"How have you been sleeping?"

"Not so good, but I've never been a great sleeper."

"On a scale of one to ten, how much worse has it been since the shooting?"

"Two."

"How's your appetite?"

"About the same."

"How are you feeling about what happened?"

"How would anyone feel if their partner was nearly killed and is lying in a hospital?"

"So, you're upset, then?"

"Wouldn't you?"

"Do you feel responsible for what happened?"

I couldn't trust this conversation to remain private. "Why would I feel it was my fault?"

"You seem defensive, Mr. Luca. There's no need to be. We're just having a chat."

I shrugged.

"You took a man's life. How do you feel about that?"

"Not good, but it was necessary. He was a proven threat."

"This the first time you shot someone?"

"Yeah."

"What was going through your mind when you did it?"

"I'm not sure much of anything."

"You shot him six times."

"I guess the training took over."

"What kind of training would that be?"

"To confront a threat with deadly force."

"Do you believe you can continue to perform the duties inherent to being a law enforcement officer?"

I had doubts but wasn't sharing them. "Why wouldn't I?"

"You have a habit of responding to a question with another question."

"Maybe you should be asking different questions."

"What kind do you believe should be asked?"

"Listen, Doc, I'm here because I have to be. I know you have a job to do, so why don't you get on with it?"

"There is no reason to be hostile, Mr. Luca."

"I'm not hostile. I'm trying to cooperate."

"Excellent." He pushed up his round glasses. "Discussing our traumatic experiences has proven to help people deal with the flood of emotions such interactions force on us. I understand your reticence to expose deeply held feelings, but trust me, it will quicken the healing process."

"Derrick is the one who I want to quickly recover."

"He sustained a serious physical injury, but with the doctor's care his body will heal. What I'm referring to, and they're just as debilitating, are the mental scars from the brutality you were subjected to."

"I'm going to be fine."

"As a police officer, it's natural to man up, forcing yourself through instead of working through the trauma. These types of exposures need to be processed, or you run the risk of dealing with the residual effects the rest of your life."

I didn't need to process anything. What I needed was to see my partner at a hundred percent and to retire. Get a small, stress-free job to keep busy and make sure my family was good.

9

Lynn was slumped in a chair sleeping. I crept quietly into Derrick's room. His eyes were closed. I gently shook her, whispering, "Lynn, why don't you go home?"

She smiled and straightened up. "I don't want to leave him alone."

"Don't worry, I'll stay with him."

"You can't be here all day."

"I'll stay as long as you need me to."

"Can you give me two hours? I have errands to run, and I can swing by my mom's to see Wendy."

"Sure, how's my little cutie-pie doing?"

"Thank God she adores my mother."

"Get out of here. I'll see you later."

I settled into the chair she vacated and stared at my partner. He had a neck brace on and seemed to be breathing rapidly. Comparing his breathing to mine, I wondered whether to call for a nurse when he mumbled, "No, no, no . . ."

I got up as he opened his eyes. He looked scared. I said, "You okay?"

He sighed, "Another bad dream."

"How're you feeling?"

"Tired. Can't sleep longer than twenty minutes at a time."

"Why not? That's what you're here for, to rest."

"I keep thinking about what happened. It doesn't make sense."

"We got ambushed. There was nothing we could have done about it."

"Nah, that's bullshit. We went in there like rookies."

"Don't beat yourself up."

"I'm not."

What did he mean by that? Was he blaming me? "Look, what happened, happened. We got to go from here. Catch the bastards who did it and move on."

"Easy for you to say; I got to deal with all this."

"Hey, that's not fair, brother. I didn't get hit, but I'm hurting over what happened to you."

He mumbled. It sounded like, "Yeah, you should be."

"I didn't hear you. What did you say?"

"Nothing. Just forget it."

"No, tell me."

He fished for the call button. "Like you said, what happened, happened. So forget it."

"You need the nurse?"

"I need a pain pill."

It was a chance to get out of the room. "I'll go get a nurse."

———

JESSIE HAD RUN off to her room, and I was loading the dishwasher when Mary Ann said, "You okay?"

"Yeah, why?"

"You didn't say much over dinner."

"Sorry. I was thinking about my visit with Derrick."

"You said he was in pain. Is that what's bothering you?"

"I don't know. He seemed different."

"He's been through a lot; he'll get back to normal."

"I don't know, I think he blames me for what happened."

"That's ridiculous."

"No it's not. He thinks I had something to do with it."

"No he doesn't."

"He does."

"What makes you say that?"

"I don't know, the way he was acting toward me."

"Don't get insulted by this, but it's not about you; it's about what happened to him. It's normal for him to feel down. He's probably depressed. At first, it's all about survival. Now that he's past that, it's about getting back to normal, and he's got a long road ahead of him, if he can even get all the way back."

"You think so?"

"Yeah, he's stuck in the hospital, thinking all day long. You know what you were feeling like when you had cancer, remember?"

"You're right. I guess I was being a jerk about it."

IN BED THAT NIGHT, my thoughts kept coming back to whether Derrick held me responsible. Mary Ann had a good point about getting down in the dumps when you were faced with a long recovery. But this felt like something more.

My ability to read people was a strong suit of mine. What was more difficult was reading myself. I felt guilty. There was no denying it. The question was whether it was rooted in reality.

IA had a point regarding the appropriateness of meeting the informant where we did. It was certainly debatable. But having us go in together wouldn't have changed things and might have gotten us both shot. I was slowly getting comfortable with both decisions.

However, there was no doubt I should have called for help when I heard the gunshot. If not at that point, certainly when I saw Derrick had been injured. Instead, I chose to seek revenge. It was wrong. I accepted the mistake and prayed that Derrick would fully recover.

Derrick couldn't know the series of events after he was hit. He couldn't blame me for any delay unless someone had told him. At this time, that seemed unlikely.

Internal affairs investigations were confidential. I hoped the timeline and details they pieced together weren't going to be leaked. If they did, my relationship with Derrick would never be the same.

I was also afraid that working out of the office where we had formed a professional and social bond would be a constant reminder of my screwup. The only way to fix that was to leave the department.

10

THE SUN WAS IN MY EYES AS I FISHED A FROG OUT OF THE pool. Having grabbed five hours of sleep, I felt pretty good. Was it because I had essentially made my mind up to leave the job?

Mary Ann hadn't taken me seriously, but I was. Besides the departmental bullshit, the fact was I was scared I could be the next one lying in Physicians Regional. Derrick was going to live the rest of his life dealing with the aftermath of being shot. It was something I had to avoid.

I didn't say it last night, but I was going to drive that point home over the next couple of days. Between her MS and my close call, I knew she'd worry about who'd take care of Jessie. One part I hadn't quite figured out was how to defend against moving from homicide to the safety of a desk job in the department.

I flipped the frog as far as possible and headed inside. Jessie was sitting at the kitchen table when I entered.

"Daddy is going to take you to school today."

"You are?"

"Yup. Finish your cereal."

"Don't you have to go to work?"

"I'm taking a little time off."

She put her spoon down. "But who is going to catch the people that shot Uncle Derrick?"

She was right. Who was going to do it? "The sheriff has a whole bunch of officers on the case. I'm helping as well. While you're at school, I'll be working from home."

"When are you going to get them?"

"Soon, honey, soon. Finish up; you don't want to be late."

If I retired without getting justice for Derrick, what would Jessie think of me? Was there a way I could explain things to her? I could tell her I felt the department treated me unfairly and decided to walk.

It was true, but what kind of life lesson would that be? Instead of hanging in there to clear your name, it was okay to bail out. It also seemed suddenly selfish to put myself ahead of Derrick.

But on second thought—it wasn't my choice. The sheriff had put me on leave. It's not like I asked for it.

Wondering if Jessie could understand that, I put another pod in the machine. As it started spitting out coffee, my phone rang. It was Sergeant Cisco.

"Morning, Frank."

"Morning, what's going on?"

"We got a body, and we think it's the informant Ayala."

"You sure?"

"No ID on him, but the responding officer had the picture we distributed and said it's him."

"Where'd he show up?"

"Imperial River, right in back of where the old Pewter Mug used to be."

"Who found it?"

"Some guy out kayaking early this morning."

"Sheriff know yet?"

"I gave him a heads-up right before I called you."

"I appreciate the call, bro."

"Anytime, buddy."

"Hey, as soon as you confirm it's Ayala, let me know."

It wasn't surprising to learn that Derrick's contact had been killed. The gang found out he was in contact with the cops and offed him. It was something that happened regularly. Nobody liked snitches, especially the bad guys. They made sure to deal with them harshly, both to protect themselves and as a deterrent.

The way I saw it, Ayala either had opened his mouth or thought he could earn points by telling his bosses that he was talking to the police. They could have eliminated him and ended it there. The fact they also wanted to send a message to the cops was the differentiating factor.

Whoever was piloting this crew was acting like they were operating in Mexico or El Salvador. It was a direct attack, defiance not often seen in America and never in Southwest Florida.

This was the largest threat to our way of life, and I was sidelined. Part of me wanted to jump right into it and find a way to hunt the bastards down. I was exhausted, and it hurt that the department hadn't been supportive.

But was that really it? I knew it wasn't. There was a fear I had been swallowing since standing over the shooter. Could I still be effective on the streets when it counted?

I CALLED VICTOR PEREZ, a lawyer from the local chapter of the Fraternal Order of Police.

"Mr. Perez, this is Frank Luca."

"How are you, Mr. Luca?"

"They put me on administrative leave."

"I heard. I assume you're ready for legal representation?"

"Not yet, but I have a hypothetical question for you."

"Go ahead."

"I'm supposed to meet with internal affairs this afternoon."

"I'd caution against going alone."

"If someone were retired or about to retire, would they still have to go?"

"You're not contemplating retiring, are you?"

"I've been rolling it around."

"Now is not the time. In addition to leaving under a cloud of suspicion, you'd be leaving too much on the table."

"I understand all that. I'm just wondering whether I could be compelled if I'm no longer employed by the department."

"Is there something you need to tell me?"

"No. I just want to know."

"Retiring or resigning wouldn't remove your obligation to participate in the investigation. If you refused, they'd issue a subpoena. Of course, you could refuse to answer questions under the Fifth Amendment, but unless there is some egregious behavior that I'm unaware of, I recommend that you cooperate and do so with counsel."

"I understand. Let me see how it goes today."

"That's a mistake, Mr. Luca. I can get this postponed if you engage our services."

"I'll be in touch if I need your help."

11

FROM THE OTHER SIDE OF THE TABLE, THE ROOM LOOKED different. I'd put plenty of witnesses and suspects right where I found myself. It was just thirty-six inches away from where I usually sat, but it felt like a hundred miles.

Borrowing a page from my interrogations, Detective Lacey kept me waiting in an interview room for twenty minutes before sauntering in. I had to keep my cool or this would spin out of control.

He sat across from me. It felt like a stranger had crawled into my bed. "Mr. Luca, as you know, these proceedings will be recorded."

"Got it."

"Now, let's start at the very beginning, why you went to the trailer on Santa Barbara in the first place."

"Detective Dickson and I were asked by the sheriff to assist on a narcotics case. We familiarized ourselves as best we could with the case, and since Derrick had some experience from working in DC, I relied on his suggestions on how to best help."

"Detective Dickson is the junior partner, is he not?"

"Yes."

"But you allowed him to take the lead in this case?"

"He had extensive narcotics experience: it felt like the right thing to do."

"Do you still believe it was the correct decision?"

"Look, Derrick is an excellent detective. What happened is—"

"That's enough."

My heart sped up. "You're cutting me off? Who do you think you're talking to?"

"If you stick to answering the questions, this will be easier on all of us."

I slammed a palm on the table. "You get your kicks from harassing cops?"

Lacey's stone-faced expression never changed. I wanted to bolt but knew I couldn't let the bastard get to me. "Go ahead, ask your questions, but remember to do it with the respect I've earned."

Lacey wet his lips. "I'm still waiting to understand how you ended up at the trailer."

"Derrick reached out to his informants, putting the word out that we were looking for information on what looked like a new player dealing in the county. He got a hit from a guy named Ayala."

He knew all this; it was in the case file. "Does he have a last name?"

"That is his last name."

"First name?"

"I don't know."

"You agreed to meet this Ayala in a foreign location and didn't even know his first name?"

"It was a lead that needed following."

"How did you qualify this, as you call it, lead?"

"As I understand it, he told Derrick he had information on the gang."

"You had no firsthand knowledge of what this supposed informant had to offer?"

"No."

"As the lead, that breaks protocol."

"You want to go after me for trusting a partner who has delivered for this department for over five years? Be my guest."

"Who chose to meet at the trailer?"

"Ayala."

"Letting an informant set the conditions on the location and timing increases the risk and is not a recommended course of action."

This guy needed to get out in the real world. "We were seeking his help and agreed."

"You arrive at the scene. What happened?"

"We approached the trailer. Derrick knocked on the door, but there was no answer."

"Did anyone try to call Mr. Ayala before entering?"

"No."

"Detective Dickson went into the trailer alone. Correct?"

"Yes. As he went in, I heard a noise and stood behind to check it out."

"Are you sure that is what kept you from supporting your partner?"

"I told you, something caught my attention, and I wanted to ensure the area was secure."

"You received a phone call at that time. Isn't that what distracted you?"

They knew about the call from Mary Ann. "My wife was at the doctor. She called; it was a brief call; I hung up imme-diately."

"Why would you answer at such a critical time?"

"My wife has MS, a serious disease. I, I was concerned about her. She had a recent attack and I was worried."

"You endangered your partner."

"The call didn't change anything. Maybe I would have been shot as well. Would you have liked that? Would that be better in your eyes?"

"What happened next?"

"I heard the gunshots and opened the door. I saw Derrick; he was lying there. I asked him how he was, and he said okay. Then I heard someone jumping out of a window and went to get him."

"Why didn't you call for help?"

"I just reacted. The shooter was there; he was a threat."

"Why not call as you chased him?"

Then I remembered what my marksmen trainer at the academy had said to all the recruits and repeated it: "Engaging the mouth disengages the brain. You don't talk when you're shooting or about to shoot."

"But your partner was severely wounded."

"And the shooter was at large. I had to neutralize him."

"Is that what you call shooting him in the back six times?"

"It seemed necessary to make sure I applied deadly force."

"Your decision making appears to have failed you. Again."

"Again?"

"Your lack of the proper oversight of a junior officer; your agreeing to meet at an insecure location; you shouldn't have taken your wife's call—"

"You leave my wife out of this."

"This has nothing to do with your wife and everything to do with your fitness to serve as a law enforcement officer."

"My ability to serve? Check your facts: this county has never seen solve rates like mine."

"Your past service is not the subject of this inquiry. It's your present state of mind that's being questioned."

"You may not have to worry about it too much longer. Chances are I'm retiring. I'm sick of crap like this."

How could people who put their lives on the line every day be treated without an ounce of respect? Why wasn't the stress of a deadly confrontation taken into account or even acknowledged?

Legitimate questions had to be asked when a shooting occurred. Naturally, one where an officer was injured and a civilian lost his life called for additional scrutiny, but IA acted as if I'd slaughtered a bunch of kindergartners.

12

———

Mary Ann came back into the family room after brushing Jessie's hair, and I said, "You read to her. I'm too frigging aggravated to do it tonight."

"I wouldn't let you do it in the mood you're in."

"What are you talking about?"

"You didn't say two words during dinner. Jessica was trying to tell you about the trip to the zoo, and you could care less."

"Me? What about you? You didn't eat anything."

"It was so tense, I couldn't."

"Oh, come on, I was thinking about the IA—"

"You're not thinking, you're obsessing."

"You know what these bastards are trying to do to me?"

"I know it's tough, but you've been a bear since it happened."

"Oh, so I'm supposed to act like everything is normal?"

"Forget it. Okay?"

"No, I can't forget it."

"Well try faking it, then. You know damn well the stress you're creating is not good for Jessica or my MS."

"Sorry."

Mary Ann retreated to Jessie's bedroom, and I went to the closet to get another bottle of wine.

DERRICK HAD BEEN MOVED to a regular room and was close to being released. It was good to see him in a chair.

"How you doing?"

"Good. I can't wait to get out of this place."

"Lynn said you'd be getting out at the end of the week."

"I'm ready now."

"How's the shoulder feeling?"

"It only hurts when I move it."

He seemed normal, like he wasn't holding anything against me. "Sorry, man."

"It's not that bad. But the doctor said I may need another surgery in a couple months."

"And the lung?"

"They say with the breathing exercises, I'll get back to about seventy percent capacity on it."

"Sorry."

"No problem, that's why God gave us two of them. Hey, Cisco said they brought a detective down from Lee."

"Yeah, guy named Kessler. He's a newbie, came from Cape Coral. Chester wanted two, but Lee could only spare one. Good luck trying to do it alone when you don't know the lay of the land."

"What's going on with IA?"

"Busting my balls like there's no tomorrow. Lacey, man, I'll tell you, I don't know why he ever became a cop in the first place. It's like his mission is to catch us doing something wrong."

"The sarge said he was pushing to get you suspended. I couldn't believe it. Why?"

"I shot the bastard too many times for the frigging handbook."

"When I get out of here, I'm going to go down to the cemetery and pump a few rounds into that bastard's grave."

"They're up my ass about why we went to the meetup in the first place. Said it wasn't secure and as the senior detective I should've known better."

"It's easy in hindsight. We had no idea who the hell was behind the dealing."

He wasn't holding a grudge. "I'm sick of the bullshit, and I gotta tell you, I'm really considering packing it in."

"Retiring?"

"Yeah."

"You can't. You love what you do."

"Yeah, well, it's hard to do the job when you get no support."

"Who's gonna get the guys who ambushed me if you retire?"

I couldn't tell him that I wondered the same thing. "Chester will figure something out."

"We can't let them get away with this. My baby almost lost her father."

"Look, right now, you get your tail out of here, and then we'll worry about the rest. Okay?"

"Can you do me a favor and hold off making any decisions?"

Though I couldn't promise it, I said yes. It was a good visit, and I wasn't going to spoil it.

SLEEPING WAS BECOMING MORE DIFFICULT. I rolled out of bed at ten in the morning and went to make a cup of coffee. Mary Ann was swimming her laps. I flicked on the TV and put on *The Phantom Menace*. I'd watched the first three *Star Wars* movies last night and would run through the rest before the day was over.

On my second mug, Mary Ann came in with a towel wrapped around her. "What are you doing?"

"Watching a movie."

"You have a doctor's appointment in half an hour."

"I know."

"You're not taking a shower?"

"I'm not going."

"What do you mean, you're not going?"

"Just what I said, I'm not going. It's just a routine checkup."

"You forgetting you had cancer?"

"Get off my back, will you?"

"If you don't give a damn about what happens to you, that's fine, but remember you have a daughter."

"I know damn well I have a daughter."

"Oh, I don't think you do. You're behaving like a spoiled brat."

"Yeah? You're not the one being dragged through the mud."

"Maybe not, but you're pulling this family down; that's what you're doing."

She stormed out, slamming the door to the garage. I heard her pull the car out and went back to my movie. Nobody understood what it was like for me. My reputation was getting trampled. How did she expect me to react?

A half hour later, I heard the garage door open. Mary Ann was back. She came in quietly. Making her way to the bedroom, she had her hand on the wall. I said, "What's the matter?"

"I'm dizzy."

"Hold on, let me help you."

She leaned on me, and I walked her to our room. "Tell me what's going on?"

"My legs are all pins and needles."

Hearing that triggered a remembrance of something I'd read online: feeling pins and needles with or without dizziness was a sign of a coming MS attack.

"I'm going to call the neurologist."

I told the nurse what Mary Ann was experiencing. She believed Mary Ann was experiencing a flare-up and told us to come right in. Before helping Mary Ann to the car, I made another call, to another doctor.

13

———————

TEN YEARS AGO, IF SOMEBODY WOULD HAVE TOLD ME I would look forward to talking things over with a psychiatrist, I would have had them committed. It may have been the way Dr. Bruno handled me, or maybe my issues were the type that could be solved in a session or two, but I didn't care, it worked.

It wasn't something I shared, but, ringing the bell, I hoped in a couple of years I'd be able to recommend seeing someone like Dr. Bruno. When the door opened, I was greeted with the smell of freshly baked cookies.

Bruno was wearing a dark blue pants suit and a welcoming smile. "Come in, Mr. Luca."

"Thanks for seeing me on such short notice."

"Glad that I had an opening that worked for you."

She led me to a pair of gray club chairs and we settled in.

"I read about the shooting you were involved in. How is your partner?"

"He's doing better. He should be released from the hospital in a day or so."

"That's wonderful. Did you want to discuss the experience?"

"No. Uh, I guess so. Everything's kind of related."

"Tell me about it."

"I handled Derrick getting shot pretty well, I thought. But the department—you see, every shooting, especially one like this, there's an investigation, to make sure an officer acted properly. But they're putting me through the wringer, and I guess I'm not handling it the best."

"They're scrutinizing your actions?"

"That's an understatement."

"Is there something you did that is a cause for concern?"

"We were ambushed, for God's sake. How about a bit of damn compassion for someone who's busted his ass for the county and did a damn good job, if I say so myself?"

"It sounds like you feel betrayed. Is that how you feel?"

"That's the right word for it. I've done everything they asked of me and more, but I'm being treated like a regular guy."

"You feel you should get special treatment?"

I did but said, "Not really, but the way the questions are posed, they're accusatory. I don't think it's right."

"You seem defensive."

I shrugged. "I love my job, but I'm thinking of packing it in."

"Retiring?"

"Yeah. I don't need the stress. It's affecting me. I didn't realize it, but since I'm on admin leave, I've been home a lot, and, well, I've not been myself."

"Can you explain in what way?"

"I'm kind of angry, and Mary Ann said the tension levels are off the charts. And her MS flared up. I feel guilty because all the stress I created caused it."

"I'm sorry she's not feeling well."

"I know it's my fault. I've really been paying attention to how you said to handle things, but this shooting, it just threw me . . ."

"Don't be so hard on yourself. Between your wife's diagnosis and the trauma you experienced, it's quite normal to react the way you did."

Now I knew why I liked talking to her. "I guess so."

"I know so. The important thing is, you recognized things were going wrong and you reached out to correct it."

"But it took an MS attack to realize it."

"That's fine. Many people wouldn't accept the responsibility as you clearly have."

I shrugged.

"Tell me about the shooting incident."

"You mean everything that happened?"

"No, just how you feel about what happened to your partner."

"I feel terrible about it. I was so afraid he'd die."

"Do you feel responsible for what took place?"

"I'm the lead, so he's my responsibility."

"Is there anything you believe that could have been done to prevent it?"

"We should have vetted the informant more deeply, and we shouldn't have agreed to meet at the trailer."

"Is that hindsight talking or an admission that you didn't follow protocol?"

"It didn't appear warranted at the time, so we ran with it."

"Are these the issues that your superiors are probing?"

"There's nothing they're not questioning."

"You mentioned you're considering retiring. Is the fact your partner was injured the reason?"

"It is. I mean, we're close friends now. He's my daughter's godfather, and I almost got him killed."

"I know you feel responsible, but unless you're withholding a critical detail, I don't see how you could have prevented an ambush."

"No, I'm not hiding anything."

"When he was hit, how did you feel about that?"

"It was surreal. Things slowed down, you know. He was laying there, bleeding, and I got so scared. Then I heard the shooter jump out a window and ran him down. I shot him dead."

"How did you feel about killing him?"

"At first, I was just on autopilot. I emptied my gun. I would have kept shooting if I didn't have to reload, but he was dead. Then I went to help Derrick."

"Shooting him felt good?"

I nodded.

"Like obtaining revenge for injuring your partner?"

"Yeah, but like I say, the best revenge is the one that goes too far."

"I'll have to remember that one. It sounds like you might believe you took it to an unreasonable extreme."

There was no way I was telling her about the last two shots. "It's possible. I fired too many rounds, but he was armed and had just shot Derrick. I didn't really think about it when it was happening, but when I realized I'd killed him, well, the good feeling that I'd gotten him disappeared. Later on, it sank in that I'd taken a life, and it's not good walking around knowing that."

"Have you ever had to shoot someone before?"

"No. It was the first time I fired my weapon in all the years on the job."

"That's remarkable."

"Not really. Despite all the stuff you see in TV shows, the far majority of cops never shoot a gun outside of the range."

"That's interesting." She crossed her legs. "I can see how using your weapon for the first time would elevate the emotional impact of such an event. Do you feel any remorse or guilt over the loss of life?"

"I mean, I replayed this over and over, and, sure, I wish I could have stopped him another way, but the training kicked in. It was almost like I was watching it instead of doing it. You know what I mean?"

"Yes, it's common to feel like an observer rather than a participant. Are you experiencing any feelings of guilt?"

"Like I said, I felt bad for taking a life, but I really believe it was unavoidable. I acted out of instinct."

"So you're moving forward, accepting a certain responsibility for your role in ending a man's life without powerful feelings of guilt?"

"I guess so."

"You're not sure?"

"Well, I was handling it pretty good considering what happened, but when IA starting treating me the way they did, it made me feel like, you know, like I did something wrong."

"It's natural to have doubts about the actions you took in such a serious event. If you believe you were justified, what I'd like you to concentrate on is getting comfortable with that belief, despite what others may say. Ultimately, it's your feeling that counts. Confirmation from others may be be nice, but they are completely unnecessary."

14

The sun was high in the sky when I came back home.
Mary Ann wasn't in the kitchen or the lanai. I went into the master. The curtains were drawn. Mary Ann was on the bed with her eyes closed.

"Frank?"

"Yeah, how you feeling?"

She whispered, "Bad headache."

"Any better than this morning?"

"A little bit. I can't take the brightness."

That was tough to avoid in Florida. "Just rest. I'll be out back."

"How did your appointment go?"

"Good. I didn't realize how much stuff is running around in my head."

"I'm glad she's helping you."

"I'm sorry for being such a jerk and causing you stress. I should have known better."

"It's okay. We'll get through this."

I bent over and kissed her cheek. "Love you. Feel better."

My cell rang. It was Dr. Bilotti.

"Hey, Doc, how's it going?"

"Pretty good. How are you doing?"

"You know, I'm doing better than I have been the last couple of days."

"Good. Look, I went to see Derrick, and he said you were thinking of retiring. What's going on?"

"I'm not exactly happy with the bullshit they're giving me, and it just feels like it might be time to call it a career."

"Retiring is long term. The IA investigation is short term. You sure you understand the difference?"

"Of course. I know this IA thing will end, but I hear they're pushing to suspend me."

"Again, if it happened, it would be for a short period of time."

"Maybe, but I don't think I could go back to work like nothing happened."

"You love your job and you're damn good at it. Don't let your ego get in the way. You'll feel good telling them to screw off when you hand your papers in, but trust me, that high isn't going to last."

"Maybe, but don't forget, Mary Ann has MS and I'd—"

"I'm not downplaying her condition or its impact on your family, but don't start making decisions by mixing things up."

"I'm not doing that; it's just a factor, that's all."

"I'm sorry, Frank, but you certainly are. Before the shooting, you never thought about retiring, did you?"

"Sometimes I did."

"We all do but not seriously. What would you do if you quit the force?"

"I've been thinking of hanging a shingle out as an investigator."

"A private eye?"

"Why not? I have the contacts and could work out of the house."

"I don't see you taking pictures of somebody's wife and her boyfriend."

"I wouldn't take those cases. Besides, I could always get a cushy job doing corporate security."

"Look, you're under a lot of pressure. Please don't make a decision now on something as important as your career. Let things settle down, then revisit it. You know I'm always available to discuss anything."

"I know. I appreciate what you're saying. Believe me, it means a lot to me."

Bilotti was right. Making a decision under pressure increased the chances I'd make a mistake. I understood that, but the idea of packing it in had a foothold in my head. The other alluring aspect of quitting and becoming a PI was the opportunity to look into who was behind the ambush.

I headed inside. After peeping in on Mary Ann, I went to the den that served as a home office. It seemed like more than enough space to run an operation from. If it grew and I needed an assistant, I'd have to rent office space, but until then I could work out of here and keep my eye on Mary Ann.

My mind ruminated over life after leaving the department as I made an iced coffee. I headed back to the lanai wondering how chasing down the people behind the ambush would be different as a private investigator than as a detective. It was bound to be harder.

If I could somehow get back on the force, I'd not only have the resources of the sheriff's department to pull from but could count on the support of fellow officers who'd be pumped to nail someone who wounded a brother.

But could I overcome feeling betrayed? It was guaranteed that someone would second-guess every move I made.

As a police officer, I could reach out to other departments and agencies for information and assistance. Throughout my career, in New Jersey and now Florida, I'd built a decent network of contacts. Some of them would resist helping me as a private investigator. It was a natural territorial thing. Even I rarely assisted them and only those who were ex-cops I knew personally.

The sheriff was tough to read. Would he order the department to limit contact with me if I retired? That would be dangerous. I had friends in every area. But Chester was a politician, and if I could help him in a case, he'd have to take the assist. The problem for him was who got the credit for it.

If I was operating outside the department and bagged the ambush leader, Chester would look bad. But if we came to an agreement, he could parade around claiming he used every available resource to keep the county safe. It would be a win for him and earn me currency to get help on other cases.

Just how would I go about catching the bastards who shot Derrick? As I thought about it, there was nothing I would have to do that was outside of what I did every day before I was put on leave. It would feel weird going private, but the investigatory skills were the same.

Moving closer to a decision, I knew I'd have to talk it over more with Mary Ann. With the stress-related MS attack she was dealing with, it made no sense to bring it up now.

Then there was Bilotti. I had to make sure he knew it wasn't going to be a rash decision. I had an appointment to see the sheriff in the morning. I was going to feel him out on going private. It'd buy me time and provide insight into how he'd react.

15

CHESTER'S SHIRT HUNG OFF HIM LIKE IT WAS MADE OF cardboard. It was overstarched, matching his manner.

"Coffee?"

"No thanks, had my limit already."

"How are you doing, Frank?"

"I'm okay."

"We hear Derrick's getting out tomorrow."

"Thank God."

"He's a lucky man."

I didn't agree with the assessment. My partner had a metal rod in his neck, a damaged lung, and spinal pain. "It was too close a call."

"We're going to get whoever was responsible for this attack."

"How is the investigation going?"

"It's slow, but we've been able to get some manpower help from Lee County."

"I heard Detective Kessler was brought down. Anybody else?"

"Not yet." He picked up a folder. "I wanted to discuss the internal affairs investigation."

"Okay."

"Now, you have to remember this is taking place outside of my oversight. Though they work for the office, a strict separation exists with a noninterference agreement guiding all interaction. I'd like nothing more than to step in and sort this out between us, but I'm prohibited. You understand that?"

"Some of it, but the style and accusatory tone is, pardon my French, bullshit."

"Unfortunately, they tend to be insensitive. But we can't discount the important role they play in keeping the public trust in our department."

"There has to be a better way to do it. Where are they with this?"

He slapped the folder on the desk. "They're recommending suspension."

"That's a frigging joke."

"No, Frank. This is as serious as it gets."

Maybe it was because I was close to retiring, or maybe it was because of what Dr. Bruno said, but the idea of a suspension didn't tick me off as much. "And the reasoning to sideline me?"

"It boils down to fitness for duty. They believe the number of shots fired was excessive and the last two shots proof of a loss of control."

"These guys make me laugh. They sit in a damn office and judge me? How the hell would they react if they were attacked? So I emptied my rounds into the punk who shot my partner. That makes me unfit? Give me a break."

"Calm down, Frank. I know these investigations can be clinical in nature, but you should know that the county psychiatrist questioned your suitability as well."

"Yeah, he's so good a shrink that he works for the county. He's another loser."

"Are we going to be able to discuss this as professionals?"

"Sorry to be so emotional, sir, but let me ask you, do you think I acted improperly? You know as much as anybody and were on the streets for a while. What's your opinion?"

"Let me break this down. On the number of shots fired, I trust your judgment in eliminating a real threat; however, shooting a fleeing suspect in the back never looks good. If the information on the last two shots leaks, it would complicate our relationship with the public. It would reinforce the belief that the police are trigger happy."

I glossed over the last rounds. "These are dangerous people we're dealing with. He may have been running, but you can't say he wouldn't have shot someone else."

"That's true."

"You think a suspension is in order?"

"Honestly speaking, I'm on the fence. Though there are mitigating factors, you showed a lack of judgment and control. We have to take these incidents seriously . . ."

He let "seriously" hang in the air. "The department should take the shooting of one of its own seriously. It should take the invasion of a brutal gang into our county seriously. That's what should be happening, instead of coming after me."

"Nobody is coming after you, Frank."

"Really? Then why aren't I out there hunting these bastards down?"

"You were involved in the incident. Protocol prevents you from being involved in the case."

"You can waive that."

"As much as I'd like to, we can't interfere. You know that."

"You won't have to." I held my forefinger and thumb a hair apart. "I'm this close to retiring."

"I'll assume that's not a threat."

"It's not."

"Good. Now, don't act rashly, Frank."

"I'm not. In fact, I've given it a lot of thought. What would you say if I told you I was thinking of becoming a private investigator?"

He scrunched his face. "You? A private eye?"

"That's right. I could help the department with this case."

"We can't compensate someone outside the agency."

"I know. But if my actions prove critical in nailing whoever it was, I could get the reward money."

"This is a crazy scheme, Frank. I can't believe you're even considering something like this."

"Let me ask you one question: would the department share information with me if I worked the case privately?"

"I'm not prepared to discuss something like this."

16

LYNN GREETED ME AT THE DOOR AND PUT A FINGER TO HER lips. "The baby's sleeping."

She looked tired, but her worry lines had receded. I hugged her, whispering, "How are you?"

"Better, now that Derrick's home."

"He feels good?"

"He's weak and in pain. Right after we got home, he slept for three hours."

"You think he's up for a visit?"

"If it was anybody else, I'd say no. Come on."

We walked through their family room and I spied the playpen. "Let me take a peek at Wendy."

A smile erupted on my face as I looked at their baby. As we headed to the bedroom, I whispered, "She's precious."

The TV was on but Derrick's eyes were closed. I wanted to let him sleep, but Lynn nudged him awake.

"How ya doing, buddy?"

He couldn't move his head. "Happy I'm home, I can tell you. Lynn, mute the TV."

The baby started crying, and Lynn left to tend to her. I said, "Wendy is getting big. Last time I saw her was three weeks ago, and she looks like a different kid."

"I know. I remember you telling me how quickly Jessie changed."

"Enjoy the ride. Before you know it, she'll be asking for the car keys."

"I don't know if I'll ever be ready for that."

Among a handful of pill bottles sat a spirometer to exercise your lungs. "Trust me, no one is. How's your breathing going?"

"I'm at sixty percent in the bad lung, ninety-four in the other one."

"Do what they say to do, and they'll bounce back. I hated to do the breathing thing when I was in the hospital, but it works."

He frowned. "What's going on with IA?"

I shook my head. "It looks definite that they're going to suspend me."

"That's crazy."

"I'm sick of the BS, man."

"Hang in there. You can't bail out on me."

"You should be going on disability with the issues you have."

"I don't know, I'm way too young to sit around."

"Maybe if I open up a PI office, you can come work with me."

"I'm not ready for something like that."

"What about corporate security work? I have a couple of contacts I can tap."

"I need time for all this to sink in, Frank. Who knows, maybe in a little while, after the bastards who did this are behind bars, I'll think differently."

"Take your time. I just want you to know I'm looking at options."

"Got you. How's Kessler doing with the investigation?"

"From what I hear, it's slow going."

Derrick pointed to the TV. "Geez, look at this."

The headline read: "Fourteen-Year-Old East Lee County High Schooler Dead of Overdose." I put the sound back on.

A reporter was standing in front of the school. A half-staffed flag blew in the background as he said, "The body of the young girl, a cheerleader for the Jaguars, was found by a group of students just after noon today. The Lee County Sheriff's Office and medical examiner are on the scene. Though it's unconfirmed, sources tell us she suffered a cardiac event due to drug use."

I shook my head. "A fourteen-year-old? What the hell is going on?"

Derrick struggled to prop himself up. "This has gone too far. We need to call a national emergency or something. Mobilize the entire country; put the army at the border; whatever it takes."

"I agree. but we also need to find a way to reduce demand."

He was gasping for breath. "Where the hell does a kid get this crap from?"

I grabbed the remote and shut the TV off. "Don't get worked up, bro. You need to rest and get back on your feet."

"It just pisses me off to no end."

"Me too, but you have to take it easy."

"I know, but it could be our daughters one day."

"They're going to be fine. Look, you take care of yourself. I'll stop over tomorrow if you're up to it."

I WAS SITTING at the kitchen table with my laptop when Mary Ann came out of the bedroom. "How was Derrick?"

"Better than I expected. But he got himself riled up over that kid who OD'd in Lee."

"That was horrible. How did this happen at school?"

I didn't want her to worry about Jessica. I said, "The high school was in Lehigh Acres. You know it can be rough up there. How are you feeling?"

"Much better."

"Good. Just take it easy."

"I was going to take a swim."

"You sure?"

"I want to keep it going."

One of the traits I loved about Mary Ann was her will to push herself despite roadblocks. But this seemed dangerous. "Missing a couple of days is not going to hurt you."

"I'll take it easy. Just a couple of laps."

"Please don't overdo it."

She left to get changed, and I went back to filling out an application. When it was done, I printed it out and signed it. After addressing an envelope, I looked for the checkbook but couldn't find it.

"Mary Ann! Where's the checkbook?"

She came into the kitchen, opening a drawer. "Here it is."

"Thanks."

She picked up the application. "What's this?"

"It's to take the test to be a private investigator."

"You said you were going to think about all this."

"I am. It's just the test part. It takes a while to get it after you pass. I figured if I decide to go ahead with it, I'll save time."

She raised her eyebrows.

"It's not a done deal. I'd never make the decision alone."

"I hope so."

"Don't worry, I would never do that. I'm just trying to be prepared."

I followed her to the lanai to keep an eye on her.

17

___

A SMALL BUT PLEASURABLE BENEFIT OF BEING ON LEAVE WAS the chance to catch up on reading. It was something I loved to do but rarely found time for. I had the distinct feeling I'd made a mistake with the first book on my list. When UPS delivered the Amazon package, I thought it was something for Mary Ann.

It wasn't. The Leonardo da Vinci book was a door stopper. I settled into a chaise and began reading. Right after learning that Leonardo's last name, Vinci, was actually the town he was born in, my phone rang. It was Bilotti.

"Hey, Doc, what's going on?"

"Just received a call for help from the Lee coroner. They're bogged down with the girl who overdosed and three deaths from a house fire. And now they just found a male body and want me to do the autopsy."

"Geez, what the hell is going on up there?"

"From what he told me, based upon tattoos, the dead man was a member of MS-13. I figured you'd want to know about it."

"You think it might be related to the ambush?"

"I don't know. The MS-13 connection could be a coincidence, but you like to say coincidences rarely happen, they're generally evidence of a pattern. Did I get that right?"

"Yeah, wise guy. There an ID yet on the corpse?"

"No, he had nothing on him."

"Okay. Thanks for the heads-up."

"No problem. How are you doing otherwise?"

"I've been better."

"What's going on?"

"Had a meeting with Chester, and it looks like they're going to suspend me."

"Sorry to hear that."

"It's all right. I'm probably going to pack it in."

"And do what?"

"I'm going to see how it goes as a private investigator."

"That would be a mistake."

"What's the matter with going private?"

"It's not what you'd do, it's the timing. Making a decision of this magnitude with the pressure you're under increases the odds you'd be making a mistake."

"Thanks, Doc, but I've given it a lot of thought."

"It sounds like you've made a decision."

"I'm getting close."

"Look, I know you don't have to, but could we talk this over before you make it final?"

"Sure."

"Thanks. Look, I'll let you know what I find when I examine the body."

I'D FALLEN asleep reading and woke up hearing Mary Ann call out my name. "Frank, get up! Something happened in Atlanta!"

"What? Atlanta?"

She clicked the lanai TV on. "There was a terror attack. They set off a bomb at the airport, inside the domestic terminal, by Delta."

The da Vinci book fell onto the deck as I jumped off the chaise. "Holy shit. Who was behind it?"

"An Iranian group claimed responsibility."

I stood in front of the TV. Split screens of blown windows from the outside and destruction of the interior of the terminal stunned me. Seeing the headline that four were killed and thirty more injured, I said, "Those bastards."

"They said they were planning more attacks across the country."

"Could be just trying to scare everybody." The headline changed to "Massive Manhunt Underway to Catch Bombers." "I can't believe they didn't blow themselves up like they usually do."

"They must have set them off remotely."

A picture of streets in Atlanta lined with FBI and police officers filled the screen as the newsman said the airport had been closed along with all major arteries to and from the city.

I said it with more conviction than I felt, "They won't get away with this."

"I can't imagine being there. Those poor people."

My phone rang. It was Derrick. As we talked about what happened at Hartsfield-Jackson Airport, the president came on the screen. I hung up and listened to him assure the nation that whoever perpetrated the attack would face justice. Though they were vastly different events, I found myself wishing Chester had taken the same public position as the president.

Ears glued to my phone and eyes on the TV, the afternoon melted into evening.

Before the night was over, the FBI issued a warning concerning a possible attack in Miami. The airport there was emptied and shut down to allow time to put robust security measures in place.

It felt like September 11, 2001, when the attack on the twin towers happened. An acidic mix of fear, anger, and surrealism kept me up waiting on the crazy hope that this was just a bad movie.

* * *

AFTER SERGEANT CISCO and I talked about the bombing, he said, "We've got every officer on twelve-hour shifts, three days on, one off. Any time off is canceled. We can't take any chances."

"You helping out with Ft. Myers Airport?"

"No, Lee's covering that, but we have Naples Airport under control. By the way, they called back Kessler."

Though I figured they might, and it was justified, it still angered me. "I hope they hang the bastards and fast."

"You and me, brother."

"Man, I wish we had you and Derrick around."

"You guys will be all right. Do me a favor and push the clowns in IA out to the street. Give 'em a dirty post for me."

"Done that already, it's all hands on deck."

My phone vibrated. "Good. Look, I'm getting a call from Bilotti. I'll talk to you later." I switched calls.

"Hey, Doc, sorry, I was on the phone with Cisco."

"No problem. With the terror attack and everything, I

never had the opportunity to tell you about the autopsy. You have time?"

"More than I care to think about."

"It was a classic gang assassination, a close-range nine-millimeter shot to the base of the skull."

"MS-13?"

"Yes, we got an ID, another illegal from El Salvador by the name of Fernando Sola. A thirty-year-old from Quito."

"You think this has anything to do with the ambush?"

"I only dissect them; putting the puzzle together is your job."

"Not anymore, it isn't."

"I want you to hear me out a second, okay?"

"About what?"

"Given the bombing and uncertainty, the focus and manpower response are straining resources."

"Cisco told me everybody is on twelve-hour shifts."

"Exactly. Why don't you approach the sheriff and see about getting back to duty?"

"Are you crazy?"

"Not at all. He needs you now. The world isn't stopping just because of the Atlanta attack."

"What about IA and the suspension bullshit?"

"All back burner now."

"Maybe. But I'm not going crawling to him on my knees. He wants me, he knows where to find me."

18

THOUGH THE FBI HAD JUST KILLED THE ATLANTA BOMBER, the nation remained high strung. Feelings of relief, mine included, quickly faded. They were replaced with the fear more operatives were about to spring into action, killing and maiming Americans out of a twisted belief.

Not being behind the scenes had turned me into a news junkie. The problem was the continual recycling of the same story accompanied by endless speculation by supposed experts. Mary Ann was on my back about my obsessive watching, and since she was due home in a little while, I shut the TV off.

I grabbed the da Vinci book and went out on the lanai. Reading about how curious Leonardo was and the studies he undertook made him feel more like a scientist than an artist. His fascination would move from subjects as varied as water, human muscles, and the way light is reflected, but not before he mastered the material.

Reading about the hundreds of inventions da Vinci came up with, my phone rang. I was so fascinated that he'd thought of helicopters in the fifteenth century that I gave a thought to letting it go to voice mail. I peeked at the phone. It was the sheriff.

I dog-eared a page. "Hello, sir."

"Hello, Frank. How are you and the family?

"We're all good."

"Glad to hear. Do you have some time this afternoon to talk?"

"I think so. Is this about the IA investigation?"

"Not exactly. Let's discuss this in person, say, an hour from now?"

"I'm going to be suspended, right?"

"Absolutely not. I want to get you back to work. I'll tell you what I'm thinking when you get here."

Hanging up, my elation melted into indignation. A week ago I was expendable, and now that the terror attack had stretched the department to its limits, I was essential. It had nothing to do with my skill set or years of loyal service. Warm bodies were in short supply, and I'd plug a hole.

Mary Ann came in the door with a bag of groceries. As I helped unload the car, I said, "Just got off the phone with Chester."

She turned around and looked in my eyes. "You're getting suspended?"

"Nope, he wants me to get back to work."

"Oh, that's great, Frank."

"I don't know."

"What do you mean?"

"It just proves I don't mean a thing to them."

"How can you say that? He wants you back on active duty."

"Only because they're in the middle of a shitstorm and need help."

"You don't know that."

"Bullshit! What do you think? He finally grew a pair of balls and stood up to IA?"

Mary Ann's face whitened. I said, "I'm sorry, got a little carried away there. You okay?"

She turned around, leaving me to empty the bags.

AFTER PARKING, I sat in the Cherokee reminding myself what was important. Several items were at odds with each other as far as going back to work was concerned.

My family topped the list. That meant doing everything I could to keep Mary Ann's health strong and making sure Jessie was safe and would have the opportunity to pursue her dreams. Continuing to work for the department would eliminate stress in the house and provide a steady income.

My career was in the middle of the list, seesawing from positive to negative. I loved chasing down bad guys; it gave me a larger purpose in life. But could I go back to work for a department that seemed hell-bent on mistreating officers when push came to shove? And Chester, he had the spine of an eel when it came to defending the people who worked for him.

The thing that really gnawed at me was the feeling that I had no control. I was nothing more than a pawn they decided to put on the board again. They rolled over me, threatening to suspend me on the flimsiest of nonsense, but now that they needed me, I was expected to thank them?

Did they believe I was so hard up that I'd crawl back as soon as they said the word? My pride had been wounded, but it was dangerous to let that guide a decision.

But what about integrity? How could I teach Jessie about

the importance of staying true to your principles if I went back?

I wanted to show them I could make it without them, that I was independent. How good would it feel to start up a private practice and stick it in their faces? It would be difficult to get something started, but there weren't many private investigators in town and none with a former detective running it.

I'd probably have to take cases from Lee County to make it work. There was no shortage of cheating spouses between the two counties and a number of business disputes to get inserted into. If things got tough, I could get involved with personal injury and worker's comp claims.

Knowing there would be no middle-of-the-night calls as a private eye, I shut the car off and headed to see the sheriff. Walking to my old building, I reminded myself to tell the sheriff I wasn't coming back until I talked it over with Mary Ann.

I said hello to a couple of officers who were rushing down the hallway. There were a lot of empty desks in the bullpen, but the noise level was higher than normal. I took a peek in my old office and my stomach turned.

Going up the stairs, an officer on the way down almost knocked me over. "Whoa. Watch it."

"Sorry, Frank. Rushing to Golden Gate High, a young girl died from an overdose."

"What?"

"A kid, just a freshman, was found under the bleachers."

Bile sprayed the back of my throat. I shook my head and trudged up the stairs.

19

———

Walking into the house, I knew I had to tell my wife a different version of my conversation with the sheriff. It might not be totally truthful, but it was my duty to protect her from stress.

She said, "Did everything go well?"

Her doe-eyed look confirmed my need to doctor the story. "Yep. Chester wants me back."

"What did you say?"

"I told him yes."

Her face relaxed. "Oh, thank God, Frank."

I nodded.

"It's what you want, isn't it?"

What I wanted to do was give Chester a hard time, tell him that I was going into business and he could take the job and shove it.

That was the plan, but hearing about the girl dying from drugs changed my mind. Snapping photos of a guy cheating on his wife when our children were being threatened was something I'd regret. I had to put my selfishness behind the greater need to do what I could to protect my community.

"Yes, I just didn't expect it, that's all."

"What did he say?"

"A bunch of mumbo jumbo."

"What about Internal Affairs?"

"He said they could make any recommendation they wanted, but he claims to have told them he wouldn't implement it."

"That was good of him."

"I just wish he would have said that earlier."

She wrapped her arms around me. "I'm so happy it all worked out."

"I told you not to worry."

"I know."

"It's not all good news though."

She stiffened and pulled away from me. "What?"

"A fifteen-year-old girl at Golden Gate High died of an overdose."

She gasped. "Oh my God, how terrible. The poor baby, her family, what a waste."

"I know. Chester wanted me to start right then and there, but I told him I'd report in the morning."

———

ATTENDING an autopsy was something I usually did. You never knew what would develop during one, and the ability to ask questions proved valuable over the years. That said, I had zero interest in being there when Bilotti dissected the latest drug overdose victim.

Using the excuse that I had reinstatement paperwork to do and a backlog of emails, I waited until it was completed to head to the medical examiner's office.

I swung off Domestic Parkway into the lot of the one-story building. Before I got out of the Cherokee, I pulled on the sweater I kept in the back seat.

As I passed the autopsy suites, I buttoned my sports jacket. You had to turn off your emotions as a homicide detective, especially when it came to this place. This victim was too close to home for me. I took a deep breath before knocking on Bilotti's door.

"Frank, come on in."

Classical music was playing in the background. The medical examiner took his readers off and we shook hands.

"Is that new?" I pointed to a stand holding an old corkscrew.

"Yes. Linda saw it on Pinterest and hunted one down for me. It's from the thirties."

"That's so cool."

"Yeah, but nothing beats a simple waiter's one."

"They're good."

"I have to tell you how glad I am that you're back. You had me worried there."

"To be honest, Doc, I'm a little conflicted about returning to duty. It's hard to ignore how I was treated."

"I understand, but you can't let it bother you. You've got important work to do here." He smiled. "Besides, most of the people in the county have a high opinion of you, and that even includes me."

"I wish they would have said something."

"A couple of us did."

"You did? To who? Chester?"

"That's right. I saw the sheriff at a budget meeting and told him I didn't believe you were being treated fairly."

"What did he say?"

"Not much. He just thanked me for stating my opinion."

"I appreciate it, Doc. You didn't have to do it."

"That's where you're wrong. I had to say something. We're friends and colleagues, but that's not why I spoke up. I spoke up because they were wrong."

"Thanks."

"My pleasure." He reached for a file on the corner of his desk. "Let's go over the Wray case."

"A drug overdose, right?"

"Yes. A toxic mixture of cocaine, heroin, and fentanyl."

"The kid was taking fentanyl?"

"Not directly. It appears that the cocaine mix she was using had been cut with fentanyl. She may have been unaware that she was consuming such a powerful analgesic."

"A what?"

"A painkiller. Fentanyl is the leading reason we have so many overdose deaths today."

"Cocaine is not enough anymore?"

"The dealers add fentanyl because of the intense euphoria the combination has on users."

"But they're killing their users with it."

"Not enough deaths to offset new users who get hooked on the addictive mixture."

"I think that's what the lab said. They found traces of it in the envelope I found where Derrick was shot."

"Fentanyl is a synthetic compound similar to heroin but fifty to a hundred times more powerful."

"Hang on a second." I sent a text to the lab to confirm if the concoction was the same. "You know, almost all of this crap is coming in from China. We have to find a way to shut these pipelines down."

"They're even using the post office to get it into the country. With millions of packages, it's nearly impossible to stop it."

"If we got some cooperation with the Chinese, we'd put a

major dent in supplies. They don't give two damns what happens here. I'll bet they're frigging cheering."

"Maybe, but their people aren't immune to addiction."

"Anyway, you think there was foul play in the OD?"

"I see no evidence of that. She consumed the drugs nasally."

"Her heart gave out?"

"No, fentanyl interferes with your breathing by fooling receptors in the brain stem. It slows down the respiratory system and shuts off the body's CO_2 warning system. It causes pulmonary edema, a buildup of fluid in the lungs."

I shook my head. "Time of death?"

"Between eleven a.m. and one p.m."

"She lost her life trying to get high during lunch."

"These kids don't understand the danger they're placing themselves in."

A text notification sounded. It was the lab. The mixture matched. The deadly compounds were probably being supplied by whoever ordered the ambush.

20

THERE WAS NO NEED FOR ADDITIONAL MOTIVATION TO NAIL the bastards who ambushed us, but I got it. The percentage of fentanyl in the drugs taken by both of the girls who overdosed matched what was found at the trailer.

It was the biggest case of my career. I needed to avenge Derrick's shooting and do what I could to keep the children of my community safe. Their parents played a larger role in their safety, but it was my responsibility to make the availability of evil as scarce as possible.

My limited experience with narcotics was not going to deter me. I was sticking to fundamentals, and that started with talking to Melissa Wray's family and friends.

Speaking with her parents was difficult. I didn't expect to get actionable information and didn't. But I got what I wanted: the names of two friends the parents didn't like.

Both of them were sitting at a table outside of a triangular building that used to be a Dairy Queen. It now housed a taco joint by the name of Turco Tacos. The girls were busy working on a plate of tacos.

"Hello, ladies. We spoke on the phone. I'm Frank Luca."

The blond, who had so many piercings she looked like she'd fallen into a tackle box, said, "Hi, I'm Nancy Seagate."

"Nice to meet you."

The other girl, who had a full-sleeve tattoo on her right arm, kept eating. I said, "You must be Joan."

She nodded, her mouth full of food.

I lowered my voice. "Thanks for seeing me. I'm sorry for your loss. It must be hard on you."

Nancy's eyes teared up, but Joan just shrugged.

"I need your help. Melissa was killed by the drugs she was sold. We have to stop this from happening again. Anything you tell me stays with me. No one will know we talked, not your parents, teachers, or friends. Nobody."

Nancy said, "What do you want to know?"

"Who she bought her stuff from."

Joan said, "We don't know."

"Did you know she was using?"

A pair of shrugs meant yes. "How long was she doing it?"

Joan said, "A lot of kids at school, like, party from time to time. It's not a big deal."

"That's where you're wrong. Your friend died from it."

"That's not what I meant."

"Tell me, what did you mean?"

"Just that, like, it's been going on for, like, years. And this is the only thing that happened, you know."

"Another girl, a freshman at Lehigh Senior High, who was just fourteen, died about a week ago from an overdose."

"But up there, that's, like, a bad area."

"Trust me, good neighborhoods aren't exempt. Look at Melissa. I don't care what you do as long as you're safe. These dealers are putting poisons in the stuff they sell. They want to hook you, but the crap they're using kills. Don't you see all the ODs around the country?"

Nancy said, "We don't do that stuff. We don't know anything. Really, we don't."

"She's right. We'd like to help you but . . ."

She picked up her taco and bit into it. I wanted to knock it out of her hands.

"This is as serious as it gets, ladies. Here's my card. If you think of anything, please call me. You could be saving lives."

They stared at me. "I promise it will be completely confidential. Please, for Melissa's sake, think about this."

Driving back to my office, I found myself wondering what Jessie would look like in five years. There was no way she'd have a bunch of piercings or tattoos at fifteen.

People could do what they wanted once they were adults. Kids like this might think it's cool to decorate their bodies, but they also might regret it later on in life.

It was disappointing that Melissa's friends gave me nothing actionable, but I could work on the backgrounds of both the shooter and informant as well as track down Peter Gist, the friend of the man whose father owned the trailer where Derrick was shot.

An attempt on the life of a law enforcement officer would get any man a long sentence, but unless we could get someone to say the order came from above, it would be impossible to hang a conspiracy to murder on anyone not present.

The shooter and people like him were some of the worst people on earth, but putting them behind bars would have a fleeting effect at best. We needed to take down the leadership to make a difference and send a message that attacks on officers would be met with the full wrath of the department.

It was possible that whoever supplied the drugs that killed Melissa Wray also orchestrated or played a role in the ambush. If we could establish a chain from the street dealer who sold it to her, we had a chance to try and pin a murder rap on the leadership of the organization.

The state had recently revised a law making fentanyl, heroin, and cocaine murder weapons. It was a tough charge to make, but the rise in overdose deaths had prosecutors beginning to use the law as a deterrent. It seemed tailor-made for this case, if we could put it all together.

Back at my desk, I pulled up a picture of the shooter. I studied Gustavo Flores's eyes. There was nothing behind them. They were cold, empty of life. How could God create people without feelings?

Flores's face was marred by tattoos. On his forehead he had one of Jesus Christ, giving the impression he was a religious person. The problem was that there was an *M* in the crown and an *S* in Jesus's beard.

It was a weird mixture that law enforcement knew meant he was a member of the MS-13 gang. Since it was figured out, the gang had begun to refrain from having its members tattooed in visible places.

The Lee County detective had received a summary of Flores's record in El Salvador. He was nasty. The gang member had served six years for murdering three men. I reread it. Only six years? What kind of a justice system did El Salvador have?

A quick Google search revealed that in recent years sentencing had changed. A series of corrupt governments had been replaced with one that had no choice but to respond. The increasing violence of gangs was so bad that one out of five El Salvadorans had left the country. Longer sentences were now handed out, attempting to reverse El Salvador's descent into chaos.

A headline touting a two-hundred-year sentence for a

group of gang members was a symbol that I hoped meant the tide, if not turned, had been stemmed. I tooled around, and everything I read made it appear to be an uphill battle for El Salvador.

It was weird not discussing things like this with Derrick. I missed him and the team we'd become. Rooting around the neighborhood where Flores was rumored to live wasn't the safest thing to do alone, but with the threat of additional terror strikes, there simply wasn't any extra manpower.

21

———

A GROUP OF YELLOW-CINDER-BLOCK BUILDINGS OFF OF EAST Terry Road was home to many illegals. Most of them were working hard as landscapers, but criminals liked to live there too.

All the small apartments were shared by too many people, but that made it affordable for those looking to save money and move on. It was a place where documentation wasn't needed, just a recommendation from someone in the community.

There were three doors in building number nine. Spanish music was coming from the gravel driveway where a man was leaned over, working on a car. He picked his head out of the engine area, saw me, and ducked back to work. I approached him. He was dark-skinned with Indian features, possibly a Central American.

"Do you know Gustavo Flores?"

He shook his head. "No, no."

"Are you sure?"

"I just fix car. No live here."

"Relax. I'm not with Immigration."

I went to the center door. A woman's voice was yelling. I pounded the door until it was opened by a short lady in a green sweat suit. Over her shoulder I saw a semicircle of kids watching cartoons in a room with mattresses on the floor. I knew the flag hanging on the wall was El Salvadoran because of an officer who was crazy about their soccer team.

"Ma'am, I'm with the sheriff's office. All I'm looking for is information on a man who used to live here."

She had a silver cross hanging around her neck. "I no speak English."

"That's okay." I pulled out a picture of Flores and handed it to her. Her eyes lit up, but she handed it back, shaking her head no.

"I know you know this man."

She shook her head.

"Gustavo Flores. He's dead."

She looked at her flip-flops.

"I need to know how he came to live here. Who did he know?"

"I no want him. He a gang man. But Hector, he says Gustavo no more in gang, that he changed. I no want him, but Hector, he says we need the money."

"Is Hector your husband?"

"Yes."

"He's working?"

She looked down again.

"It's okay, I'm not going to make trouble for him. I don't care if they're brothers, I just want to know about Flores."

"He work at the Crawford's."

Crawford Landscaping was one of the larger companies that kept the tropical vegetation at bay. I pulled her husband's last name out of her and told her to wait as I went to the Cherokee. I opened the hatchback, took a couple of plastic badges and coloring books that the community office had made up and gave them to the kids.

The effort to show children the police were on their side was a good one. It wasn't easy but was necessary. The day would quickly come when we'd have to pull from their generation to keep the forces at full strength.

I waited until late afternoon to head east. Driving on Immokalee Road, I passed the entrance to Twin Eagles and made a right onto Crawford's property. It was an immense piece of land, part tree nursery, part parking lot for scores of trucks and equipment, all in the company's trademark red color.

Crews were returning from a day of work in the heat. The largely male, Hispanic workforce's long pants and shirts were sweat-stained. As I approached an older white male, a handful of workers scattered.

I introduced myself and told him I needed to speak to Hector but that he wasn't in trouble. The crew chief didn't seem to care either way and shouted out in Spanish.

All eyes were on a short man with a floppy hat as he shuffled over. We stepped to the side and I said, "You're not in any trouble. I just need some information about a man who stayed in your apartment."

He frowned. "Gustavo?"

His English was good. "Yes. How long was he with you?"

"Maybe three months."

"How did you come to know him?"

"A friend said he'd come from El Salvador to get away from the gangs. I was afraid, but he said he was done with the gang life and had been born again."

"He said he was religious?"

"Yes, in my country the only way out of gang is to die or to dedicate yourself to Jesus."

I didn't believe that gangs bowed to anyone, including Jesus. From what we knew, the only way out was death.

"Who introduced you to him?"

"Pastor Pedro at the Amigos en Cristo at the Hope Church."

———

HOPE LUTHERAN CHURCH was on a large piece of property on Old 41. I parked and walked to the Always Learning Hope Center. It was shaded by a canopy of oak trees. Spanish was being spoken as I pulled open the door.

The roomful of seniors quieted as I stepped in. A bearded man stood and smiled. He said something in Spanish and came over. We shook hands, and Pastor Pedro suggested we step outside.

We sat at a metal picnic table. I said, "As I mentioned on the phone, I'm interested in Gustavo Flores."

The pastor frowned. "We were saddened to learn of his return to a life of crime."

I wasn't sure he had ever stopped being a criminal. "Did you bring Flores into the country?"

He stroked his beard but remained silent.

"Look, I don't care about illegal crossings. I'm trying to piece together who and why my partner was ambushed."

"We don't bring anyone in. We work with sister churches to deliver people of God from the violence they're surrounded by. It's a crisis in many Central American countries, and we consider it our duty to assist."

"It's an admirable goal, but Flores was a member of the MS-13 gang."

"We were told he disavowed gang life and had been born again."

"Explain that to me. It's the second time I heard something like that. Frankly, it sounds ridiculous that gangs would let a member leave by saying they found God."

"It's true. Of course, they can't just say it. They must live it. Gangs are a tight-knit social organization, much like the church. The gangs respect that similarity. When a member decides he has had enough, he joins a church, an evangelistic one. The church provides support to the lost souls and gives them a measure of structure and, importantly, sucks up their free time with activities. They also help to find jobs for them, not easy given the facial tattoos many of them have."

"How did you come in contact with him?"

"There are many churches that help refugees when they arrive, but former gang members present a challenge, and we're one of the few who do what we can. In most cases, the member seeking to change would tell the church where they had family or a contact and then give them a church that would help them. Mr. Flores called me: it's as simple as that."

"So Flores calls you, then what?"

"I met with him, right here, in this building. He professed his love of our Lord and Savior and said he needed help. We put him up at the Flamingo Motel and found him a place to live. Unfortunately, because of the facial tattoos, it was very difficult to find a job for him. The only thing we could find was a dishwasher position at Iguana Mia."

"He worked there?"

He shook his head. "No, he refused the job."

"What then?"

"He said he had a contact to get a job. I think it was in construction."

"And you never checked?"

"You have to understand that we can't force people to do anything."

"But you knew Flores was dangerous."

"He said he'd found God."

"Did he attend services?"

"No, but there are many ways to display your love for God."

"He gets here, and you don't monitor his activities?"

"We can't possibly monitor everything people do. We thought he was doing well because he was paying the rent and seemed to keep out of trouble."

22

DRIVING BACK, I TRIED TO UNDERSTAND HOW THIS patchwork system claimed to be doing good. I understood trying to help legitimate cases where people were in dangerous situations or simply wanted a chance for a better life. But as a law enforcement officer, my belief was in using legal means to come here.

As far as helping gang members, former or otherwise, melt into our society, that could have merit, but, damn, where was the oversight? Who knew how many criminals had snuck into the country claiming they had gone straight?

And even if they were truthful about trying to stay out of a life of crime, the statistics were against them. Florida's five-year recidivism, lower than the national average, was an appalling 65 percent. I'm all for giving people a second chance, but without supervision it was doomed to fail, just like Flores did.

It pissed me off that because of the help of well-intentioned but ignorant people, my partner had taken a bullet. We relied on the public for help, and they were a valuable resource, but this was an area where they had no idea of the implications of their actions.

Driving on Airport Pulling Road, I passed Spanky's Speakeasy when a robbery-in-progress call came across the radio. Two armed men had stormed into Dylan's Drafthouse. It was two blocks away.

I hesitated before responding. A handful of cars were in Dylan's parking lot. Stomach clenched, I slid out of the Cherokee. Drawing my weapon, the smell of mildew hit me. I was overcome with the feeling I would have to kill again.

Creeping to the front door, I forced myself to focus. A male was guarding a dozen people lying on the floor. Another armed male was taking jewelry and cash from the patrons. I took a breath and burst into the bar.

"Drop your weapons!"

Heart pounding, I held my pistol with both hands. I was dead certain I'd have to fire. My finger starting pulling the trigger as the man guarding the patrons moved his arm. The one holding the gun.

To my relief, he tossed the gun aside and put his hands in the air. The other thief complied as well.

"Get on the floor! Facedown!"

Putting a knee on one robber's back, I slapped cuffs on him. As I did the same to his partner, I surveyed those on the floor. Was there another conspirator lying among them?

A man wearing jeans and a T-shirt began getting on his feet. "Get back on the floor!"

"I gotta take a leak, man."

"You stay where you are!"

"I gotta go bad."

"I don't care if you pee in your pants. Don't move."

Calling for assistance, two uniformed officers, guns drawn, entered. I nearly collapsed from exhaustion before identifying myself. Refraining from hugging my support, I summarized the situation and retreated to the restroom.

My hands shook as I locked the stall. I sat on the bowl and took deep breaths, thankful that the situation had been peacefully resolved. Though I was a wreck, I took solace in the fact that I was in control of my tactical decision making and had diffused a volatile situation without firing my weapon.

Before we were done here, and with the required paperwork, I'd miss dinner. I sent a text to Mary Ann to let her know I would miss dinner but would call her as soon as I could.

***

"Sorry, I didn't think it'd be this late."

"It's okay. Did you eat?"

"Not really."

"I'll make you a sandwich. Turkey?"

"Sure. I'm going to jump in the shower."

"Before you eat?"

"Yeah, I was sweating like crazy when it went down, and can't stand my own smell."

"I'm sorry."

"It's okay, but you know, that was the first time since the ambush that I faced danger."

"It wasn't that long ago. You have to be careful, Frank."

"I gotta tell you, it was nerve wracking. I really thought I'd have to shoot someone. I mean, there were two of them, and both were armed."

"Why did you go in? You should have called for backup."

"I don't know. Maybe I had something to prove—"

"Prove? To who, the sheriff?"

"No, me."

"That's ridiculous and dangerous. You could have gotten hurt."

"You know it's part of what we do."

"Maybe you should retire like you said you wanted. Maybe I was wrong to worry about you making a career change."

"I don't know, I'm pretty sure, for the time being anyway, that I'm doing what I'm supposed to be doing. Maybe after all this is over, we'll see what's what."

"You better be extra careful, then. We need you."

"Don't worry. Let me get cleaned up."

I didn't want to tell her that I had to deal with whatever scourge was infiltrating our little piece of paradise. Though it couldn't be completely eliminated, I was hoping to push it far enough back so our daughter would have less of a chance to get caught up in it.

23

THE BRIEFING ROOM WAS STANDING ROOM ONLY. ANYONE NOT patrolling was anxious to hear the sheriff's update.

"I'd like to thank everyone for coming and especially for your diligence. You've made sacrifices to keep our county safe and made a real difference.

"Homeland Security issued a new report this morning. They reduced the threat level to blue, a guarded risk of an attack. Though not definitive, they are reasonably confident that law enforcement agencies can reduce their elevated public profiles to a more normal presence.

"That said, they continue recommending we remain vigilant. In consideration of the lesser threat, I'm going to begin moving the department back to normal. The transition will happen over the next two months, provided we don't have an event."

As Chester babbled about time off, I wondered if he would have brought me back if he knew the ramp-up in security was going to be dialed back. I told myself it wasn't worth wasting energy over as I had a full plate on my hands.

With the change in terror status, it might be possible I

could get help tracking down the ambusher and drug kingpin. I thought about organizing a surveillance operation.

The problem was identifying exactly who to observe. As Chester finished up, an idea came to me. As we filed out of the room, I pulled Sergeant Cisco aside.

"I need your help to nail the guys who shot Derrick."

"Whatever you need. How can I help?"

"At this point, I'm unable to get a lead onto who's behind it, and frankly it's going to take a while, especially on my own."

"Tell me, what can we do?"

"I want to shake the trees. Round up users and street dealers. I don't care if their small time or not. Arrest them if they're in possession or have an outstanding ticket. Be creative."

"You want to squeeze 'em to see if they know anything?"

"Not the users. I want to send a message to the dealers by bringing them in. But we can use the opportunity to tell them just how damn dangerous the crap they're taking is.

"Let's hope they get the message."

"Probably not, but if just one does, I'm a happy camper."

"One's better than none."

I nodded. "And I'm going to ask Chester to see if he can get the Lee sheriff on board."

"Sounds like a plan. When do you want us to start hauling them in?"

"No time like the present. Kick it off tonight."

"I can't broadcast it though. The guys are going to bitch about the paperwork, but maybe we'll bring in a dozen a day. Would that work?"

"Sure. Tell them to focus on hardcore users if they know who they are and anyone who's high school age."

We had eight males and two females as overnight guests of the county. When I strolled into the holding pen the next morning, the officers smirked. They knew what I was doing.

Looking over the list of arrests, I focused on possession amounts and repeat offenders. We had two street dealers behind bars, both caught selling. They were the quickest path to information.

The users, I'd let go through the system. They'd get fined and hopefully scared or embarrassed enough to quit. I had both dealers cuffed and brought to separate interrogation rooms.

Standing outside the overnight cells, I searched the faces of the arrested. Some were scared, others desperate, or hopeless. A surge of sympathy mixed with disgust welled up in my belly. Facing one set of cells, I said, "Listen up! You're going to be arraigned in a bit. The judge will probably let you go on your own recognizance, and then you'll be stuck in the maze we call the system. Lawyers, court appearance, fines, a record, basically a total time suck and stain on your life."

I turned around, facing the other cells. "You may get off without serving any time, but I can assure you of one thing, you keep using the crap being peddled out there, and I'll have a good chance of seeing you again. But it won't be here, it'll be at the morgue. The stuff they're dealing is deadly." Walking away, I repeated, "Don't make a mistake and end up dead. Don't do it."

The skinny kid in room three was Willie Bickoff. He was twenty-eight, and it was his first offense. As a newbie, he was my best shot. File in hand, I swept into the room.

"Mr. Bickoff, I'm Detective Luca. You're in a pretty deep hole, my friend."

He was scared and shrugged.

"This is your first offense. It's a damn serious one, but there's a chance we could help each other out here."

He straightened up. "I hope so."

"I'm not going to record this interview just yet. See if we can find a way to work this out."

"Sure."

"I'm looking for information on who is dealing the stuff laced with fentanyl."

"I don't know."

"Come on now. You expect me to believe that? Think again. Sometimes it's labeled with two capital *Cs*."

His eyes shifted. "I really don't know."

I stood up. "That's a shame. Because I could tell the prosecutors the evidence of you selling had somehow disappeared."

"Hold on."

"Start talking."

"Look, I really don't know, but just being here, if it gets out I said anything, I'll end up dead like the other guys did. You don't know how brutal these guys are."

He was wrong. I knew too well. "Think about it some more. You've got about an hour for your memory to improve."

24

———

Yesterday's haul temporarily cleaned up the streets, but neither dealer provided any actionable information. I reviewed the night's arrests, zeroing in on a dealer with an outstanding warrant for driving with a suspended license.

Samuel Scott was thirty-four with a lengthy rap sheet, most of it for selling meth. Scott had his first encounter with the law before he turned twenty. Here was a classic example of why the three-strikes law needed an adjustment. Under the present law, only violent crimes triggered mandatory sentencing guidelines.

It seemed to me that drug dealing needed its own maximum number of offenses to trigger a larger sentence. Technically, it was not considered violent, but anyone who lost a loved one to an overdose would disagree.

Breezing into the room, I announced myself and sat down. The florescent lights bounced off Scott's shaved head as I sized him up. He was muscular and had good teeth. At least he'd shown the smarts to lay off the crap he sold. It was a good sign.

"You've been here so often, this place is like a second home to you."

He shrugged. "I never stay long enough."

"Your problem is, no matter how good your lawyers are, you're going to be behind bars for a while."

Scott shifted in his chair.

"You've got an outstanding warrant for driving with a suspended license and for the third time. That means up to five years in jail, Sammy boy."

"Five years? You shitting me?"

"That's the law. Judge's hands are tied."

"Oh, come on, man."

"I could help. If you feed me some information, there's a chance the warrant notice was overlooked at booking."

"What do you want?"

"Who's the new guy selling coke laced with fentanyl?"

Fear flashed across his face. "I don't know nothing about that shit."

"Really? You've been around a long time, frankly too long, but that's another story. And you're trying to tell me you don't know anything?"

"I keep my fucking head down, man."

I stood up. "That's a shame. You'll be arraigned later today."

"Hey, hold on a minute, man."

"You got something for me?"

"Take it easy."

"As soon as you start feeding me, I'll calm down. Start talking or I'm out of here."

"Look, I don't know too much, man, but I know the motherfuckers are brutal. Word gets out I opened up, and my ass is as good as dead."

"Nobody is going to find out. Tell me what you know."

"Just that they're, like, trying to go corporate, you know?"

"What do you mean by that?"

"Just that they only want to flip high-price rocks. Their own mix. Nothing else."

I hadn't even thought of the selling price of drugs. "What else you know?"

"Nothing. That's it, man."

"Sorry, Sammy, that's not enough. You don't give me more, you're going to be inside a long time."

"All right, man. Look, the only other thing is, I hear they got a trap house in Everglades City."

"You've been there?"

"No, man."

"Exactly where is it?"

"I don't know."

"You expect me to believe that?"

"It's true, man. I got no idea."

"What about the initials *CC*? What does it mean?"

"It's their brand, man. Like I said, they're like Apple."

"Who's running this thing?"

"I don't know, but I heard he's some kinda business guy."

"Who is he?"

"All I know is they call him The Professor."

I TOOK the stairs two at a time to my office. Pressing Scott hadn't produced any more information. What I had was flimsy, but it was a pair of leads to follow.

I grabbed the phone. "Cisco, it's Frank."

"Hey, Luca, what's up?"

"Does the nickname The Professor mean anything to you?"

"The Professor? No. I mean, I remember back a couple years ago at Gulf Coast U, this guy was impersonating a professor, but that's not what you're looking for, right?"

"Yeah, I got a possible lead on the guy leading the drug gang. Supposedly, they call him The Professor."

"It doesn't ring a bell, but I'll ask around. You never know."

"All right. What about any drug houses in Everglades City?"

"Everglades? That's out of the way. I've never run into anything down there."

"Okay. Check around on that as well."

"Will do."

I put the nickname in the system. Eight hits. Four males and two females had been arrested for financial crimes and none were within ten years. There was also the impersonator that Cisco had recalled. The last one was an adjunct professor at Florida State who had been arrested for exposing himself.

It was a long shot, considering the mystery man could have never been arrested. Maybe the nickname was wrong or recently acquired. I couldn't put too much focus on it. What I could do was chase down the Everglades City angle.

Sitting on a sliver of land at the mouth of the Barron River, Everglades City had once been the seat of the county. Nowadays, it was better known as a place to take airboat rides and fish.

There were only four hundred people who called it home, and the average income was less than half that of Naples. About an hour away, it was a remote and unlikely place for the operations center of a drug gang.

However, what someone would gain by the cover

provided by such an improbable location was offset by a sparse population.

In small communities, the goings-on were well known. I felt any newcomers, especially a drug-related enterprise, would stick out. Then again, the former mayor had gotten away with stealing money from the town for ten years.

Picking up the phone, I called the current mayor. The phone rang six times.

"Mayor Ballard's office."

"This is Detective Luca with the Collier Sheriff's Office. I'd like to speak to the mayor."

"You got him. How can I help you?"

"I'm interested in anything you can tell me about newcomers living in Everglades City."

"We ain't had many new folks moving here. But we got ourselves a bunch of folks who rent their places out, you know, tourists and all."

"Have you or anyone seen anything unusual?"

"What exactly are you looking for, son?"

"I'm looking into a rumor, and that's all it is at this point, about a drug gang that might be operating out of your city."

"A drug gang? In Everglades City? I don't think so."

"Any suspicious people in town?"

"This is the Everglades. We got all kinds of folks passing through."

"How about anyone with facial tattoos?"

"That sounds like it hurts. I would've remembered seeing someone like that."

"You know anyone with a nickname of The Professor?"

"No, sir."

"Thank you, Mayor Ballard. If you happen to see or hear of anything, I'd appreciate it if you'd give me a call."

After giving him my contact details, I hung up. We had

patrol cars that passed through the area to show a presence and to keep the speeders on the desolate roads from killing themselves. I needed to see if they had noticed anyone that looked like a gang member or was suspicious. I also needed to put them on the lookout.

25

A ROAR OF APPLAUSE SOUNDED AS I PERUSED THE PREVIOUS day's arrests. My face broke into a smile. Derrick was in the building. I went into the hallway. It was lined with officers. My partner was smiling as he was wheeled toward our office.

I hoped it was the neck brace that made him appear fragile, but his sports jacket also hung off his shoulders. He'd lost a lot of muscle. If he couldn't walk, he'd never get it back.

I pointed to the clock. "Hey, what do you have, bankers' hours?"

"It's good to be here."

He grunted when I hugged him. "I could certainly use the help. So hurry up!"

"It's going to be a while, if ever . . ."

"Nonsense. Take your time, buddy. Let's eat. I ordered a bunch of stuff from Bistro La Baguette."

"What, you get a raise since I've been out?"

"Nothing's too good for my partner. I got you the farmer sandwich that you like."

I handed him the baguette. "Thanks, man. What'd you get, the Niçoise salad?"

I nodded. "So how you doing?"

"Sick of rehab and bored out of my mind. But never mind me, what's going on with the case? You said you had a lead."

I filled him in on what I'd squeezed out of the arrested dealer. Derrick said, "You'd think with a name like The Professor, that'd we'd be able to track it down. But I guess because they're new, it hasn't gotten around."

"I'm going to take a ride down to Everglades City this afternoon. I've never been there."

"Me neither."

"I want to snoop around; check the area out."

"I'd love to come along."

"Believe me, I'd love to have you, but when your wife finds out, I'll be on the shit list, and you'll never see me."

"She didn't even want me to come today. Said it was too soon, and she's waiting in the parking lot for me."

"She should've come in. I feel terrible."

"I told her not to."

"I get it."

"Look, man, I'm aching to get the bastards who did this."

"Don't worry, buddy. We will. You can bank on it."

Route 41 was ruler straight as it cut through the swamplands of the Collier Seminole State Park. Other than the occasional person fishing off the side of the road, it was desolate. I passed Captain Mitch's Swampland Airboat Tours and made a right onto County Road 29.

After five miles of nothingness, the road rose. A couple of businesses appeared, scattered on land surrounded by water. The place looked like a boater's paradise or, by the number of rods sticking in the air, the place to fish.

At the end of the main road sat an old hotel named the Captain's Table. I made a right and hit what looked like the center of town. It was anchored by a white building housing city hall, and across the street was a quaint old church with a red door and tower. The sign said it was established in 1926, but architecture aside, it could have been built last year.

Just past city hall was a sprawling building with a pair of dolphins framing its name: The Rod and Gun Club. It made me think of a lodge of some sort. Maybe it was a gathering spot for fishing and shooting enthusiasts.

Besides three kids near a pizzeria advertising Gator Pies, I didn't see a single soul. I assumed the fishermen and boaters were out enjoying themselves, but the place felt deserted. Not even a car driving around. I half expected to see a tumbleweed rolling down the street.

A couple hundred yards past the Everglades City Museum was the water. I made a left and drove along a wide berth of water that was lined with docks. Half the boat slips were empty.

Homes sat on the other side of the street. A couple of expensive ones were mixed among ones that hadn't been updated in decades. They didn't share the same price range, but with the Gulf of Mexico half a mile away, they all had great views and easy access.

Eyes bouncing from the homes and boats, I was surprised by the sight of a young woman on a bicycle. It wasn't a ghost town after all. I saw a sign for an airport and followed it.

A building that looked like a California lifeguard stand was marked as the control tower. Two old prop planes sat on the side of a runway that ended at the water's edge. I wondered if any drug dealers used this. Between the water and an airport in the middle of nowhere, this area looked ideal to operate clandestinely.

Driving around, I pulled into a lot for the Everglades Bait and Tackle Shop. I parked in front of a sign advertising they sold live shrimp, pinfish, and crabs. Passing an outdoor ice chest, I pushed through the door wondering what pinfish were.

Behind the counter a guy with a T-shirt so faded I couldn't make out the logo was winding a wire around a fishing lure. He didn't pick his head up.

"Excuse me."

"Uh-huh. What you looking for?"

"Me and a couple buddies are going to have a boy's weekend, you know, fishing and drinking." I pointed to a photo on the wall where two guys were each holding a large fish. "What kind of bait you need to catch one of those?"

"Them redfish like cut mullet. You can use shrimp, but out here, they really go for mullet."

"You know, that's what a guy I saw at the dock said. This guy had tattoos on his face. I can't remember his name. You know who I'm talking about?"

"Nope."

"You know, a couple of my buddies they like to party. I mean, not all the time, but when they're away from the wives. You know any place they can get some stuff?"

He looked at me for a second before shaking his head.

"All right, I'll come back when everybody gets here." I headed for the door and turned around. "Say, you know anyone called The Professor?"

"Mister, around these parts, we do our fishing on the water."

26

Though it felt like Everglades City could be the base of operations, I couldn't get a shred of confirmation from anyone there, nor from the patrol cars that passed through daily.

I took a sip of coffee and resumed my attempt to identify who The Professor was. Though I knew it was unlikely to be helpful, I plugged the nickname into Facebook. What came up was another list of useless results.

All the euphoria I'd gotten from leaning on the drug dealer had vanished. If the information was real, it needed fleshing out. The quickest way to do that was leaning on someone, make it next to impossible for them not to cooperate. It appeared like the dealer community was scared to talk, and I couldn't blame them; there was a good chance they'd end up dead.

We could keep arresting them and hope one of them would talk, but I had a different angle to try. I grabbed my jacket and headed out.

I STOOD outside the door to the Always Learning Hope Center. A chorus of children's voices were repeating the phrase, "My name is."

A male voice said, "Good. Very good. Now, try this: I am ten years old."

I pulled the door open. Pastor Pedro was standing in front of a dozen children, pointing to the words on a chalkboard. He smiled and addressed the kids in Spanish before coming over.

"You wear a lot of hats, Pastor."

"If they don't learn English, they'll never escape poverty."

"True, but if they get mixed up taking drugs, they'll never make it to twenty."

He raised his eyebrows. "What do you mean by that?"

"Just that an effort to target and hook children on to powerful drugs is underway."

"Yes, Satan is always at work. We warn the children about the danger of drugs and addiction."

"If you want to do more than that, have a real impact by taking some of the scourge off the streets. Help me."

"In what way could I help?"

"Put me in touch with some of the gang members you helped to bring up from El Salvador."

"That would be impossible. It only works with complete confidentiality. These people need to be able to trust some-one. They come here alone. I couldn't betray the trust they place in me."

"I'm not interested in their legal status. I want to know what they know about gang members who didn't stay straight."

"I understand that, but, still, it's impossible. If I did that, no one would believe anything I said."

"Keep in mind, Padre, the ones who did the betraying are those that didn't toe the line. They promised their allegiance to God and didn't keep it."

"It's very difficult for some to make the transition."

"I don't care how hard it is for them. What I worry about is stopping the spread of drugs and catching the people who shot a police officer."

"I want the same things as you do. And I want to help. But breaking my promise of confidentiality would destroy what we've built."

I lowered my voice and leaned in. "If you don't help us, you'll have a lot more to worry about."

"I hope that is not a threat, Detective."

"It's not a threat. I'm just reminding you that harboring, encouraging, inducing, or being a part of a conspiracy of aiding, abetting, or simply facilitating the presence of an illegal alien is a crime."

His face went blank before he recovered. "These people just want a better life for themselves and their families."

"That's exactly what I'm trying to ensure for everyone. All I want is a community that is as drug- and crime-free as possible. I have a young daughter as well. I want the same for her as the kids inside."

"It really starts with the children, doesn't it? They can create a new, love-filled world."

"They can't do it on their own, Padre. We have to make it easier for them. You have to understand my goal isn't to send back people who came here illegally. That's not my job. You can give all the reasons why they should be allowed to stay, but you and I both know, if you don't deal with those who commit crimes, every valid reason falls apart."

"No one is irredeemable. They can find salvation in Jesus."

"I don't know much about that, but it has to start with someone wanting to change. Recognizing where they've gone wrong and making amends. Some of the people you're helping won't ever get there."

"We accept what they tell us; sometimes they disappoint us."

"I need your help. Please don't let me call for another agency's involvement. We can do this quietly. Nobody has to be told about it. You know who the bad apples are. They're the only ones I'm interested in."

Newly arrived immigrants, legal or not, had a helluva advocate in Pastor Pedro. I had my doubts he'd agree to help me. The last thing I wanted to do was throw a bunch of crap his way, but it was clear the threat was dangerous enough to warrant it.

He'd only given me one name to start with. Given the pastor's reluctance and the fact he was supposedly a former member of MS-13, I was hopeful the lead would pan out.

27

THE LAST OF THE SUN DISAPPEARED AS I PASSED THE Rookery Bay Environmental Center. Jessie had gone on a school trip and was so excited about the place that I promised to take her back. Keeping my word was about as important as family was. Since the ambush, the to-do list had swelled.

This section of Naples was twenty minutes closer to Everglades City. Was Arturo Lopez part of the drug gang? I put a baseball cap on and threw a newspaper on the dashboard.

Turning onto Henderson Creek Drive, I slowed down. To get an idea of the surroundings, I drove past my target, the ME Travel Trailer Park. At the end of the street was a wide canal brimming with brackish water.

I circled back and pulled onto Hibiscus Lane. The gravel street ran through a sea of aluminum-sided trailers. The lots they sat on left little room for the odd chair or bicycle.

The unit that Arturo Lopez shared with two others was the last one down the second lane. I didn't turn my head as I passed and made a U-turn at the end of the access road.

I made a right out of the trailer park and pulled into a Walmart on Collier Boulevard that backed up to the RV site.

Circling to the rear of the superstore, I parked next to a tractor trailer and got out. Using the Cherokee as a block, I zeroed in on Lopez's unit with my binoculars.

A pair of window air-conditioners framed a dented door. One light was on, and based on the shadowy figures, it looked like two people were inside. I kept my eyes on the trailer as I reached for my thermos.

Draining the last of my coffee, the door to the trailer swung open, banging off the wall. I put the binoculars to my eyes. Arturo Lopez was heading in my direction. I slipped behind the truck. Unless Lopez had been watching me watch him, there was no way I could have been seen.

Lopez was wearing baggy shorts, a blue T-shirt, and a baseball cap. He had so many tattoos, it looked like he'd been fire-hosed with blue ink. He checked behind him twice before crossing into Walmart's parking lot. Keeping an eye on him, I crept around the cab of the truck until he disappeared.

I hustled, following from a safe distance as he walked along Collier Boulevard. There was an Aldi ahead; maybe he was going to pick up some food. Lopez went right past the supermarket and continued walking alongside a steady stream of traffic.

A Marshalls was just ahead, but he crossed to the other side of the street. I thought he'd go into Dunkin' for a coffee but he breezed past, headed instead to a Walgreens at the Route 41 intersection.

I grabbed a newspaper as soon as I entered the pharmacy and spied Lopez at a customer service counter. He had his phone out and showed it to the clerk. She nodded and disappeared as I sorted through the battery display.

The clerk handed Lopez a FedEx envelope, and he headed for the exit, tapping his phone as he walked out. Keeping my eyes on Lopez, I waited for the cashier as a Honda swung up to the entrance. Lopez got in and the car took off.

Running outside, I watched the car turn onto Route 41 and head south. I went back in to the counter, flashing my badge.

"The man that was just in here, Arturo Lopez, he picked up a FedEx envelope. I want to know who the sender was."

"I'm sorry, sir, we can't reveal that information because of privacy laws."

I knew I'd need a subpoena, but it was worth a shot. "I'll be back with a warrant. Now, I want to see the video of the front entrance."

THE NEXT MORNING I was at my desk looking at a DMV record. The plate that was on the 2015 black Honda Accord belonged to a Cadillac Escalade that had been wrecked a week ago. Since the video footage didn't even catch the driver, it was useless.

All we knew was what I witnessed. Lopez left his place, walked to Walgreens where he picked up an envelope and left in a car with a stolen plate. Whatever Lopez was up to, he was cautious about it.

Was he working for the gang I was looking into? Or was he expressing his own criminality? I wanted to be patient, but, then again, I couldn't wait the two minutes for my electric toothbrush to finish. I put on a bulletproof vest and headed to the parking lot.

The trailer park was quiet. A double-wide near the entrance had an Office sign in a window. I rapped on the door and stood to the side. A fiftyish man with a round beer belly and smudged glasses opened the door.

"Office opens at ten."

I stuck my badge in his face. "Unit 402. I need you to go get me Arturo Lopez."

"Arturo? What he do?"

"Nothing important. Tell him I'm an insurance inspector. Let's get going."

I followed the manager to a well-kept trailer. Hand on my holster, I put my back to the unit as he knocked.

I held my breath as I heard the door opening. "Mr. Lopez, the insurance company sent an inspector. When can you make the place available?"

"Insurance?"

As he stepped outside I swung around and pointed my pistol at him. "Hands in the air."

"What are you, Immigration?"

I nodded and slapped cuffs on him.

28

———————

It was tough to look at Lopez. With all the tattoos and a two-inch scar on his chin, he was as hard as they came. Cuffed to the table, he was staring at the floor.

"Let me take those off."

Free, he crossed his arms.

"I'm Detective Luca, with the homicide division. What do you say we help each other out?"

He shook his head.

"You're an undocumented alien. Your ass will be back in El Salvador in no time if you don't cooperate."

"What do you want?"

He had a strong Spanish accent. "Information on who's behind the gang pushing the new variety of coke-fentanyl."

"I dunno nothing."

"What about the ambushing of an officer on Santa Barbara Boulevard?"

"I said, I dunno anything."

Did that mean he knew something and that it was the drug gang behind the shooting?

I stood up and picked up the cuffs. "You're heading back

home, my friend. If I were you, I'd watch my ass because I'm going to spread the word down there that you sang like Justin Bieber to the cops."

"Either way, I lose."

"No, if you help out, you walk out of here. Immigration don't have to be notified. You keep your nose clean; you got nothing to worry about."

"They find out I talked, an' they always do, and then I'm a goner."

"Depending on what you tell us, we can get you into protection."

"And what? live in, like, Montana and freeze my ass off?"

"We could tailor a placement, maybe New Mexico or somewhere nice and warm."

"You know, man, look at me. How am I gonna hide anywheres?"

"How long you think you're going to last doing what you're doing? Whether here or in El Salvador, chances are, you'll be killed or spend the rest of your life behind bars."

He shrugged.

"Look, right now, you're going to stay here until you're sent back. Why don't you help us out?"

"I don't know much."

"Whatever you can tell me is going to help you. Who's running it?"

"I don't know. You gotta understand, it's a real tight operation. Everything is separated. They're crazy paranoid."

"They have a place in Everglades City, right?"

"I think so."

"Tell me where it is."

"I don't know exactly. I never been there."

"How could that be?"

"Like I said, they keep everything separate."

"What did you do for them?"

He crossed his arms.

"I'm not going to use anything against you. This isn't being recorded."

"Some of the guys just do the pickups and get it to the street."

"Where are the pickups made?"

"All over the place."

"Give me one."

"Well, sometimes I, we get a text to go to a UPS locker or a Walgreens and get a FedEx that was sent."

"They're sending drugs with FedEx?"

"Yeah, and we get a new ID to use for the next delivery."

"You're sent a fake ID with each lot of drugs?"

"Uh-huh, almost every time with the product is a new driver's license."

"And that's the coke-fentanyl mix?"

"Yeah."

"How much are they sending each time with the couriers?"

"A hundred and ninety grams."

That was an interesting amount. At two hundred grams, the sentencing jumped from three years to seven and the fine doubled to a hundred thousand. The street value of each shipment was about twenty grand.

"How often is a shipment sent?"

"Almost every day but not to the same place."

"You do all the pickups?"

"No, me and two guys, we rotate. Sometimes I drive or deliver. All the teams do it the same way."

"How many teams do they have?"

"I don't know."

"Five, ten?"

"Something like that."

"Who is The Professor?"

His eyes darted. "I dunno."

"He's the top dog, isn't he?"

A slight nod gave me the answer.

"What do you know about him?"

"Nothing. Just he's real careful, and he don't tolerate no shit."

"What's his name?"

"I dunno."

"Come on, Arturo. You know."

"They call him The Professor."

"What's his name?"

"I dunno, all I know is I think his name is Julio."

"What about his last name?"

"I dunno."

"He from El Salvador?"

"No idea where he came from."

"Mexican?"

He shrugged.

"Do you think you can find out more information?"

"No way, man, I can't ask questions. As it is, I got to think of some bullshit to tell them about all this."

"Tell them it was Immigration. You were released and have a court date. They'll buy it; it happens all the time."

———

SINCE I'D BEEN to Everglades City with the Cherokee, I took an unmarked car this time. Working with limited information, we needed a large surveillance presence to identify the location of the drug house. The problem was, a meaningful force would be obvious in the sleepy hamlet.

Right before the bridge leading into town, I noticed a police unit parked just off the road. It was a perfect spot to nab speeders anxious to complete the boring drive. It gave me an idea about using one of the mobile watchtowers the department used to control traffic.

Loaded with cameras, it could work but would stick out. I thought about using license plate scanners; we could sort out the residents from the tourists with rental cars and focus on the balance.

There was a chance it could work. The problems were the time it would take and the possibility they used boats to get around. As I passed a building with a turret that housed a hotel called Everglades Isles, I tucked the idea away and went into observation mode.

Driving deeper into town, I passed two cars, both heading in the opposite direction. It wasn't as quiet as the first time I came, but the place still felt like an empty movie set.

The only car in the lot in front of city hall was a blue pickup. I took Hibiscus Street past the Rod and Gun Club. Several cars were parked on the grass in front. It was the busiest business in town. It had to be the best place to pick up information, but if I went in there I'd stick out like a donut display in a health food store.

The road ended at the water, and I turned onto Riverside Drive. Every dock was built alongside the road, not sticking out. With no boats in sight, it looked like everyone was out on the water.

There was no activity outside the homes opposite. I cut up Kumquat Street, away from the inlet. A yellow house with an asphalt tile roof and a sagging porch caught my eye. Three cars were parked in the rear of the house.

Without looking at the home, I drove past it. At the end of the street I made a U-turn. This time I looked. The shades were down in every window. I was a quarter mile away from the house when a UPS truck swung onto the street.

Keeping my eyes on the rearview mirror, I saw the UPS stop in front of the yellow home. The driver hopped out and jogged to the front door. What was he delivering? Drugs? We needed eyes on that house and fast.

29

ROUTE 41 HAD NARROWED TO ONE LANE. I WAS LESS THAN twenty minutes to Everglades City. Passing the East River park and launch ramp, my cell rang.

"Frank, it's Cisco."

"How you doing?"

"All right, where are you?"

"Heading to Everglades City. What's up?"

"We got a body. Two teenagers were fishing at a canal by Bear's Paw and saw the body of a male in the weeds just off Airport Pulling Road."

"Age?"

"Kids said between thirty and forty."

"You inform Dr. Bilotti?"

"Yeah. Forensics has been dispatched as well."

"Okay. I'm on my way."

THE LEFT LANE on Airport Pulling Road was closed and loaded with police vehicles. I parked behind a crime scene van and surveyed the area. Gray plastic fencing surrounded a utility substation that bordered the street and the north side of the canal.

On the other side of the water a crowd of onlookers gaped from the patio of Spanky's Speakeasy. The guardrail ended where the bridge began, replaced by a low concrete wall. You couldn't see the body from the road.

It was a good spot to dump a body. I figured whoever did it had pulled over, heaved the body over the wall and took off. It couldn't have taken more than a minute. As busy as Airport Pulling Road was, at midnight it was empty. I scanned for cameras.

I'd been to Spanky's, a *Little Rascals*-themed restaurant, and knew it closed hours before midnight. There was little chance of finding a witness. They probably had cameras, but I couldn't see them covering the other side of the waterway.

I picked out the top of Bilotti's head from a handful of people on the rocky bank of the canal. After one more look around, I headed to the uniform guarding the scene.

After signing in, I ducked under the yellow police tape. Bilotti was bent over the body, which appeared to be face-down. At the sight of a heavily tattooed arm, I hesitated.

Bilotti rose and spoke to the forensics crew. When he finished instructing them, he stepped toward me. The full body came into view. It looked too familiar.

"What do we have, Doc?"

"Male, mid to late thirties, single shot to the base of the skull. Based on the style and tattoos, I'd say it's another gang execution."

"Time of death?"

"At this point I'd estimate between one and three a.m."

When a forensic tech shifted the corpse's head, I said, "Holy shit. It's Lopez."

"Who?"

"Arturo Lopez. An illegal from El Salvador. He fed me information on the drug gang. They must have found out he talked to me and killed him."

"You're sure it's him?"

"A hundred percent." I don't know why I said it, but I did. "How the hell did they find out?"

He shrugged. "You want to go over the body now?"

"Yeah."

Examining the body with Bilotti confirmed it had been pitched over the barrier. We'd get forensic evidence, but I was betting that whatever DNA we found came from an illegal and wouldn't be on file.

I didn't get back in the Cherokee until 2 p.m., and when I did, I began questioning my role in the death of Lopez. It couldn't be because he'd talked with me. He was a gang member dealing in drugs and who knew what else. He was allied with the most violent people on the planet.

Maybe he got into an argument with someone or double-crossed the gang. He could've stolen from them. Whenever that happened, gangs always exacted swift punishment to discourage others from stealing. It was possible, but the timing was too coincidental to pass my smell test.

I tried to find another reason, but the feeling it was my fault flooded out alternatives. I'd arrested Lopez in broad daylight. At the place he was staying. Had I made a fatal mistake?

Had my eagerness for information not only led to another death but spoiled a possible source of information? Was this another example of allowing emotions to cloud my decision making?

I played tug-of-war with the rule that said to stay out of a case you were involved in. The rule was valid, and if they hadn't attacked me, there was a good chance I'd have gone along. But they pushed me, questioning my motives and integrity. Anybody would have reacted the same way.

Why hadn't I just retired? There was no stress investigating insurance fraud or employee theft. I'd be able to work from home, where Mary Ann needed me. Why hadn't I just taken the leap? How the hell was I going to nail these bastards anyway?

It was looking like a deep undercover operation was the only way. But there were challenges with that approach. Based on the separation strategy the gang operated under, it would take a long time to work someone's way to a position to nail the leadership. The other issue was simply getting in. If they used former gang members, an undercover agent would need a way to be vetted.

There was no easy answer. I couldn't wait years to catch these guys. In that time, countless people would overdose on the crap they were selling. A call over the radio broke my train of thought.

An eighty-six-year-old man with dementia had wandered away from his daughter's home and was nowhere to be found. The address was close by and I needed a distraction. I put the strobes on and hit the gas.

I turned off Airport Pulling Road before a BP gas station and onto Clipper Way. It was just a few blocks from where Lopez was dumped. I pulled up to the home where the man was last seen.

A pair of uniforms had the trunk of their vehicle open. I approached and realized a solution to catching the drug gang was staring me in the face.

<h1 align="center">30</h1>

Arturo Lopez's execution bothered me. But there was a silver lining; the brutal murder suppressed any resistance to my warrant request. It was the quickest approval I'd seen in my career. I was thankful I wasn't questioned over it.

Surveillance was a critical element of police work. I'd done it hundreds of times. But this one was different. A first for me. We were going to use two drones to capture high-resolution video of Everglades City.

Judges required exacting information on what we were looking for and where. The what was easy, it was the location that was unknown. Anyone could observe or photograph private property as long as they were on public ground.

In this case, we were in public space, but the newness of drone technology had raised privacy alarms, and thus warrants were required. I stretched the truth by stating two specific locations in the city were suspected. The reality was it could be anywhere.

Collier County had a dozen drone units. That was a lot more than most counties, and I was grateful we'd made the investment. It wouldn't be long before we had a separate unit to handle them, but at the moment officers voluntarily went for training. I wasn't a fan of video games and didn't take the offer to learn how to operate a drone.

It was something I regretted as soon as I saw the age of the two officers who strolled into my office.

"Detective Luca?"

"Yeah, you the drone masters?"

They chuckled. The shorter one, with red hair, stuck his hand out. "Joey Connolly, this is Brendan White."

"Good to meet you. Sit down."

"Hey, we're sorry about what happened to your partner. How's he doing?"

"Pretty good, he was here a couple of days ago to say hello."

"That's good. Say, we looked over the warrant; tell us what's going on."

Closing the door, I said, "We're certain this drug gang is the one that ambushed us. These guys are pros and as cautious as I've ever seen. Anyone talks, they assassinate them. That body by Spanky's, he was an informant who fed me and paid for it with his life."

"I hear these guys might be MS-13."

"We know they recruit from them. There may be an affiliation, but DEA doesn't have anything hard on it."

Connolly said, "We don't want that shit down here."

Brendan said, "No frigging way, man."

"Exactly. That's where you come in. We have info from a couple of sources that one of their bases is in Everglades City. We think it may be the main place they distribute their garbage from. You know, these guys are lacing the junk with fentanyl. It's what those two young girls OD'd on."

Brendan said, "That shit is, like, crazy powerful. They

gave it to my mom for her bone cancer, but she'd be zoned out on it."

"It's way more potent than heroin. We have to put these guys out of business. So we need to get eyes on the two locations in the warrant?"

"Well, here's the thing. While we're certain they're in Everglades City, the location, well, we're just not sure of."

The two exchanged glances, and Connolly said, "What's the plan, then?"

"Now, this may sound 'out there,' but keep in mind these are the guys who shot one of us. I still can't believe we almost lost Derrick to these thugs."

"We're gonna get them."

"No frigging doubt. Bring it on."

"You guys are the experts. What I hope you can do is monitor the entire area."

"I don't know. We'd need more than two drones for that."

I reached for some papers. "I knocked out a ton of places. Let me show you."

They were maps with the city in sections. "The ones coded green are homes where a family with school-age kids live or the residents are over seventy. It's likely that we're looking for a house that's rented, and I'm thinking closer to the water is where we need to look."

"What kind of activity are we monitoring?"

"I know it sounds sketchy, but anything out of the ordinary. Cars coming and going at odd hours. This is a quiet town, and I'm betting something is going to stand out."

By the looks on their faces, I was ready for one of them to take me up on the bet. Connolly said, "All right. I want to see if we can get some of the newer models. They fly higher, no one will know they're up there."

"How's the video from that distance?"

"You won't believe it. Crystal clear, we can even read plate numbers if we need to."

THE SUN WAS low on the horizon as redheaded Connolly and I drove toward Everglades City. We had two spiderlike drones in the back of the Cherokee. The aerial vehicles were hybrids, equipped with tiny combustion engines and generators. I was surprised at the configuration, which allowed them to extend their flying time. It was an important factor. We needed to minimize the launching and retrieval if we were to hide our presence.

We pulled into the gravel parking lot of what passed for an airport. I chose the place because it was out of the way and a natural place to see something rise from. The airstrip closed at dusk and the place was deserted.

Connolly opened up the carrying cases. He spread the arms and landing gear out, locking them into place. He checked all the connections.

The drones were more fragile-looking than the one used to locate the missing man. It also had a small fuel tank and motor instead of a battery pack. The camera seemed larger as well.

"What do you want me to do?"

"Let me open the base control program up." He grabbed a laptop out of a satchel. "You can take the units out. Set them down over there, on that patch of dirt."

"You got it."

"Place them about six feet apart. I'll be ready to go in five."

I picked one up. It weighed about twenty pounds. If this

crashed into anything it would cause damage, I thought as I put it on the ground.

Lifting the other one up, I said, "I thought they'd be lighter."

"The fuel adds a couple of pounds, but it gives us up to thirty-six hours of flying time."

"How high is it going to fly?"

"They can go as high as thirty-five hundred feet, but we'll cruise around at two thousand. Won't look like anything but a bird way up there."

31

Connolly looked over the drones one last time then backed away. "Let's get them up."

He balanced the laptop and tapped its keys. The propellers began spinning on one unit, making a high-pitched sound. As their speed increased, it got louder.

"That's too loud."

"Don't worry. No one will hear it after it goes over two hundred feet."

"Okay."

"All right, here we go."

The drone wobbled as it lifted off the ground, then stabilized, rising faster than I expected.

"I'm sending this one to the northeast." He keyed in coordinates and said, "It's on the way. Here goes the next one."

The second drone's ascent mirrored the first takeoff, and Connolly sent it to the southwest area, by the waterfront. We got back in the Cherokee.

"They'll be in position in a minute or two. Let me get the control panel and feed on your laptop."

He opened the app we'd installed earlier and clicked a

link. The screen filled with a moving image from one of the drones. He hit a drop-down menu, and a second later I was looking at split-screen feeds from both drones.

"Now remember, this control here zooms in the video. You see something you want a closer look at, just zoom in with this."

"And to move the camera, I use that controller, right?"

"Yep. Try it on this one. It's in position."

I played around for a couple of minutes, but it wasn't easy to maneuver the video feed.

"You'll get it. Just keep practicing."

He had more confidence than I did. "I hope you're right."

"I'll drive back. You keep an eye on the feeds and play around with it."

Being able to remotely monitor the areas kept us out of view, but I didn't like being at the office. If I saw something that needed checking into, I was forty-five minutes away. The plan was to come back every thirty hours. We'd land the units, check them and refuel. It would also keep us from being there the same time every day and leave the drones with six hours more flying time. A margin of safety, if needed.

***

STARING AT THE SCREEN, I realized the reality of my idea. It was a needle in a haystack ramped up by a ten factor. Sixteen hours of watching, and I had nothing but an empty bottle of eye drops and a sore neck.

There were only four hundred residents and a couple of hundred tourists and part-timers. Why wasn't anyone standing out? I stood, stretching my back, when a boat came into view.

It was coming into the body of water alongside Riverside Drive. A fishing boat with only one person on board. I zoomed in. The guy was under the canopy easing the craft toward the dock. He partially emerged, throwing a bumper over the side.

I froze. His arm was covered in tattoos. His face was obscured by the floppy hat he had on. He cut the engine, and the boat drifted toward the dock. Grabbing a coiled line, he jumped onto the mooring as it bounced into the bumper.

He tied up the boat and looked in both directions before getting back on board. Disappearing under the canopy, he came out stuffing something into a backpack. I picked up the phone to see if we had a patrol car in the area as he hopped onto the dock.

The boater took his phone out and seemed to send a text. He then walked north. After being told the nearest unit was in Carnestown, I adjusted the camera feed to capture more of a northern view. A dark blue car was turning onto Riverside Drive.

It slowed and the boater jumped in. The car sped off out of view. I fiddled, trying to get eyes on the auto, but neither camera was in range. Why hadn't I learned how to fly these damn things? And where the hell were the young turks that knew how?

This could be them. This guy wasn't fishing. He had tattoo sleeves on both arms. He'd sent a text and gotten picked up. It was the same method they used when picking up drugs at Walgreens.

Grabbing the phone, I made a call. "Connolly, I got something but I lost them. Some guy, fitting the description, came in on a boat. He didn't look like he was fishing, then he sent a text and was picked up by a car. Same MO the drug ring uses."

"Wow."

"I lost them. I couldn't follow them with the drone. You should have been here."

"You got footage, right?"

"Yeah, I just told you."

"You get a good view of the car?"

"Yeah."

"Which camera?"

"The southwest one. Why?"

"This just happened, right?"

"Of course. Why all the questions?"

"We should be able to grab the plate number. Let me jump on the recording and isolate it. I'll let you know."

"I'll be right up."

"You don't have to. I got it. After I clip it, the lab is going to have to blow it up. If they get a partial, we'll need DMV's help."

"How long is all that going to take?"

"Who knows, a couple of hours if the lab isn't backed up."

"If they give you any bullshit, let me know right away. I'll get the sheriff to put a priority on it."

"You got it."

"Call me as soon as you know something."

JESSIE and I were in the family room watching a Hallmark movie. She said, "How come you keep looking at your phone, Dad?"

"I'm sorry, honey. You know how I feel about playing with your phone when you are with people, but it's a very important work thing."

"About who shot Uncle Derrick?"

Kids were smarter than we gave them credit for. "Yes, honey, we think so."

"It's taking a long time to catch them."

I didn't need the reminder, especially from someone who considered me invincible. "We're getting close."

"Really? Like tonight?"

"I'm not sure. That's why I'm keeping an eye on the phone. It's almost time to go to bed. We'll watch the rest of the movie tomorrow."

"It's almost over. Can't I just see the ending?"

"There's another half hour to go. You'll have to wait till tomorrow. Now, give me a kiss goodnight."

"Can I read for a while?"

"Sure."

I kept my eyes glued to the phone, watching feeds from Everglades City. My eyes were straining to see if there was any suspect activity. I kept blinking to wet my eyes.

"Wake up, Frank."

Mary Ann had come home from a book club gathering.

Reaching to the floor for my phone, I said, "Uh, I must have dozed off. What time is it?"

"Nine thirty. How was Jessica?"

"Good. She went in a little while ago." My phone rang, it was Connolly. "I got to get this."

32

THE BLUE FORD FOCUS BELONGED TO BERNARD PLATT, A fifty-year-old resident of Everglades City. Platt's home was in an area known as Plantation Island, technically a part of the Big Cypress National Preserve.

Accessible by a single road, the small community wasn't being monitored by the drones. I'd discounted the possibility, believing that sitting in a national park, surrounded by marshes, was too remote an area to operate from.

We only had two drones, and I didn't want to waste one watching a handful of houses. Staring at a feed from a repositioned drone, I regretted the decision. Two heavily tattooed men were smoking at a picnic table near a canal leading to the Gulf of Mexico.

The ramshackle house sat on a plot littered with tires and two junkers on crates. I felt it drew a bit too much attention to itself, but, then again, way out in the sticks, who was looking?

Platt had one blemish on his record. A dozen years ago he was arrested for assault. When his application for a grant from FEMA was denied, he attacked the agent he felt was responsible.

It was a serious charge, landing the FEMA rep in the hospital, but it was a loss of control driven by emotion. It wasn't confirmation he was violent, but it was something to note.

We had no idea who the mystery man on the boat was. Neither man smoking outside the home was a match. We tracked down the owner of the boat from its hull number. He was sixty-two-year-old Bill Carney, who lived in a small home across from where the boat had docked.

Carney was a lifelong resident who taught at the only school in Everglades City. I couldn't see how he could be related to the drug gang. It made no sense, but I reminded myself I was in the business of sorting out senseless acts.

We were keeping one drone trained on Carney's place and the other over Platt's home. Though I wanted to drive out and start asking questions, I had to quell my impatience to develop more information. If we were going to bring the top guy down, we needed irrefutable evidence.

I FINISHED PRACTICING with the app Connolly had installed. It felt like a video game, but he said I'd develop the skills to fly the drone. Landing was altogether different, and I didn't care to learn how. All I wanted to do was to follow a target if needed.

Surveillance was the only investigative tool I was using. It seemed pointless to try and shake information from the street. There was no sense in alerting the gang, and I didn't want to be responsible for another assassination.

Time always crawled when you were waiting for something to happen. I picked up the phone.

"How you doing, buddy?"

"Hi, Frank. How are you?"

"Me? I'm good. What about you?"

"Okay. I'm a little tired right now. Just finished up with physical therapy."

"How's the pain?"

"Ah, about the same."

"Sorry, man."

"Don't worry. What are you doing?"

"Keeping eyes on a couple of people of interest."

"The ones in the Everglades?"

"Yeah. But it's—hold on, I gotta go; he's on the move."

Platt was walking to the water at the back of his house. He was carrying a black duffel bag. Platt stepped onto the small boat, untied it and started the engine. He motored around the island toward the water that ran into the Gulf of Mexico.

As I moved the drone, allowing its camera to capture Platt's movements, I wondered where he was going and what was in the bag. He moved along the canal that bordered the road to Chokoloskee Island. The island was part of Big Cypress and was home to a couple of dozen homes and tourism-related enterprises.

It was another place I initially thought as unlikely and was now another source of regret. Platt maneuvered the boat around the island. It looked like he was going to dock at a place near the tip called Captain Corey's Charters.

Platt veered away from Chokoloskee toward the open water. He was headed to the Ten Thousand Islands. I watched him weave around an island wondering if he was going to a rendezvous of some sort. If so, what chance did we have of stopping drug dealers like this that went to such lengths?

Most criminals took the path of least resistance. I always believed criminality was rooted in laziness. They didn't want to work for their money, so they'd find the easiest way to take or make some.

This gang broke the rules. They were the opposite of reckless. The planning and covertness of their operation reminded me of a serial killer who'd given me my greatest challenge. Until now.

I kept flying the drone along Platt's path, making sure it stayed behind him. The boat was heading south to the open water. It hugged the marshy land, occasionally brushing against mangroves. He was piloting a twenty-footer, so I thought he couldn't be going too far out.

Another boat came into view from the south. It was a much bigger vessel. Were they going to meet up? As the gap between them shrunk, Platt turned left, going around a land outcropping and toward a riverlike body of water.

The big boat continued north. They weren't meeting. Platt continued east, motoring through a large bay. The waterway narrowed, and I noticed a small dock sticking out.

I zoomed in on the rickety structure. It was the dock for a place called Watson's Place. It was a campground. Who the hell would camp out here? Everglades City was Las Vegas compared to this spot.

Platt eased his way to the dock and tied up. Grabbing the duffel bag, he disembarked and headed toward the campground. A younger man approached and they shook hands. Platt handed the duffel bag off and walked to the far end of the encampment.

He unzipped the opening to a large, sturdy tent and disappeared. I stared at the screen. I counted seven people, all male, in the camp. Were any of them connected to the drug gang? None of them were overly tattooed. It was impossible to determine what was going on there.

A guy carrying a sack over his shoulder approached the tent Platt was in. He stuck his head in and entered. What was happening in there? Was it an exchange of drugs for money?

33

EYES GLUED TO THE VIDEO FEED, I CALLED CONNOLLY.

"I'm going to need some help monitoring these guys. You think we can split it up and keep eyes on them twenty-four seven?"

"Sure. Between the three of us. We'll get it covered."

"Good."

"No problem."

"You're a native, right?"

"Yup, born on Capri Island, right by Marco."

"Then tell me, who the hell would go camping in the middle of nowhere?"

"Man, a lot of people go out to Watson's Place. Some of the tour guides go by there because of the history."

"What history?"

"You don't know about Bloody Ed Watson?"

"No. Who was he?"

"Around the early nineteen hundreds, he came down here. He'd killed a couple of times before but never went to jail for them. They say it was because one of them was a famous outlaw known as Belle Starr. Anyway, he came down here and bought Chatham Bend Key. He had a farm and did some trading with Key West. He made a lot of money, but he was as violent as they came. They say he hired a bunch of farmhands, and instead of paying them, he'd kill them."

"That's crazy."

"It was. Anyway, there was no proof until a hurricane blew through in 1910, and the leg of a woman who worked for him became exposed. She'd been gutted and weighed down. The town folks had enough, and thirty of them got together and shot Watson dead."

"Florida's got some crazy stories."

"Uh-huh. Let's put a plan together to split the coverage."

After dividing up the hours, I went back to watching the feed. My mind kept drifting to the story about Ed Watson. I wondered whether we were going to tie another strange story to the area.

IT WAS BEGINNING to feel like we were going to have to force something to happen.

It was the afternoon of the second day, and Platt still hadn't left the campground. This morning he'd gone to his boat and worked on the engine for a while. It appeared to be routine maintenance, as he fired it up without a hitch.

He'd left his tent several times, chatted with others on the property, and fished for a couple of hours. A couple of tour boats came close to the island but never docked. It was maddening: nothing was happening.

It wasn't much better watching Carney's home. He'd gone to the Rod and Gun Club at dinnertime yesterday, returning home before eight. The blue glow in the window meant he spent the rest of the night watching TV.

Just before eleven this morning, he walked to the convenience store. Inside of fifteen minutes, he emerged with a small bag and walked back home. I didn't know how these people lived such quiet lives. We spent a lot of time dreaming of waking up in the morning with nothing to do, but the reality of that was a boring existence.

Boats filled with fishing poles began to trickle in as the clock moved toward 3 p.m. As the stream thickened, one vessel caught my eye. It was docking behind Carney's boat. A scrawny man piloted it and another stood on the starboard side. There didn't seem to be any fishing gear aboard.

Both men wore baseball caps. As the driver reversed engines, the other man grabbed a piling and vaulted onto the dock. He waved goodbye and the boat took off.

I followed the man as he crossed Riverside Drive and walked up Jasmine Street. Passing the first house, he took his phone out and began texting. I zoomed in. He passed the Masonic Lodge and turned onto Storter Avenue.

A UPS truck slowed as it passed him, pulling over two houses ahead. The man walked by the truck and up the dirt driveway of the next house. It was a light blue home with no cars parked out front. The UPS truck rumbled away as the man went around back and into the house.

I checked the block and lot number, running it against the tax records. The home was owned by Franklin Mayhew. According to the DMV, he was sixty-four years old. He had a clean driving record and no run-ins with the law.

He was also not the man who just walked into the house. For someone to use the back entrance of a home without ringing a bell, they had to be a close relative or renters.

It was early, but it looked like we now had to keep eyes

on three places. If we zoomed out, we could use one drone for Carney's home and this one.

Playing with the camera to get as close as possible while covering both targets, a FedEx truck came into view. It turned on Jasmine and slowed approaching the Mayhew home. It stopped just past its driveway, and the driver hopped out, hustling to the blue home next door. The same one that UPS had delivered to.

As the driver made his way back to the house, a white pickup truck pulled into Carney's driveway. The driver stayed in the car. A minute later, Carney came out of the house and slid into the vehicle.

I guided the drone, following the car out of town, leaving the new target without eyes on it. I grabbed the phone.

"Cisco, it's Luca. Look, I need you to get someone to tail a white Ford pickup. It just turned onto Forty-One, heading west. Two males are in the car."

"What's going on?"

"The passenger is a person of interest, and we've had him under surveillance in relation to the drug gang. Someone we're watching used a boat owned by him."

"What do you want us to do?"

"Let me know where they're going. You have an unmarked in the area?"

"Closest is just east of Lely."

"Damn."

"If they're headed to Naples, we'll catch up to them in fifteen."

I didn't want to lose them but hated to take eyes off Everglades City. "I'm going to keep the drone on them until I can hand them off to you."

The unmarked was sitting in the parking lot of Corey Billie's Airboat Rides. I called Cisco as the pickup approached. As soon as our guys tucked behind them, I guided the drone back to Everglades City.

Zooming into Mayhew's place, I did a double take, rechecking the street name. In the twenty minutes I'd left them uncovered, things had changed. Dramatically.

34

A SILVER HYUNDAI SUV WAS PARKED ALONGSIDE MAYHEW'S house. It was on the grass, close to a hedge of viburnum, screening it from the street. Why was it parked there instead of in the shade of the oak tree by the driveway?

Zooming in the camera to grab the Hyundai's plate number, I noticed a black van with the Amazon logo rolling into view. For a small town, there were a lot of couriers making deliveries. It seemed unusual, but this place was miles from the type of shopping Americans were used to. Why drive three-quarters of an hour when web vendors could deliver in a day?

I sent a text with the plate number as the Amazon driver got out and went to the next house. He rang the bell and leaned a small carton against the door.

As the Amazon truck pulled away, the door opened. A man in jeans and a yellow shirt stuck his head out. He looked both ways before sweeping the package into the house.

It wasn't until he was back in the house that I realized his arms were covered in tattoos. I focused on the light blue home. There was a late model Ford SUV parked in the rear of the house. On the grass. It wasn't there before.

I began to doubt myself. Keeping one eye on the laptop, I pulled up the video app on my phone. Rewinding the video in slow motion, I saw the Ford SUV pull up the driveway. Two men got out. One had a bag like the one Platt had. Keeping their heads down, they walked to the entrance.

Before they got to the door, it opened. The men hustled in. I didn't get a glimpse of the person inside to see whether it was the one with tattoo sleeves.

My cell rang. It was Cisco. "What's going on?"

"The pickup pulled into Lakeside Pavilion."

"The nursing home?"

"Yeah, the one with the bad reputation."

"Did they go in?"

"Both of them did."

"Can you have your guy hang around?"

"Sure. You want Hanlon to see what's going on?"

"Hanlon's tailing them?"

"Yeah."

An Amazon van turned onto Jasmine. This street was turning into Grand Central Station. "He's good. See what he can get out of the receptionist."

I watched the houses for a minute and tapped out a text to get the owner information on the blue home. An older car came into view. It was a Lincoln. One of those huge Town Cars, and it was going slowly. I zoomed in, but it drove past the homes I was watching, making a left at the stop sign.

I rubbed my eyes and continued watching. After fifteen minutes I called Mary Ann. "How you doing?"

"Good. Getting ready to go down to the bus stop. We're going straight to dance school."

"Busy, busy. You feel okay?"

"Yeah, I'm fine. What are you doing?"

"Staring at a screen so much my eyes are going to fall out."

"Make sure you take a break. Every ten minutes look away from the screen or you'll ruin your vision."

"Really?"

"I just read something on it."

Another call was coming in. I pulled the phone away from my ear. It was Cisco. "I'm sorry, I got to get this call."

I flopped calls and Cisco said, "Frank, Hanlon talked to the front desk. They said Carney's mother just moved in there."

"His mother? She must be ancient."

"I don't know, but they said she used to live with him but it got too much for him."

"Carney's mother lived with him? In the Everglades house?"

"I don't know where it was."

"Who was the other man?"

"His brother."

"Do me a favor and have Hanlon talk to Carney. If his mother was living there, I can't see it being a drug house."

"No problem. I'll tell him to wait until they end their visit."

"Okay. Also, Carney has a boat. I want to know who was using it two days ago."

I rolled the revelation around. Carney might have been part of a crew that used his house for their drug trade despite the fact his elderly mother lived there.

Carney didn't have a record and had been a teacher and lifelong resident. Unless he was taking role playing to the stars, it didn't fit that his mother was in a cheap nursing home. If he was a good enough son to have his mother live with him and was involved with drugs, you'd think he'd use some of the money to put her in a top-notch place.

Besides, we had nothing but his boat being used by the suspicious man picked up by Platt. There could be a simple explanation for allowing someone to use it. Or he could be being paid handsomely by a dealer looking to put distance between them.

The benefit of eliminating Carney was watered down since it now looked like we had another house to watch. I stretched my legs and sat back down as a text came in.

The Hyundai belonged to Alice Wright. It was registered to an address in Cape Coral. Typing her name to find out if she had a record, Cisco called again.

"Frank, Hanlon just talked to Carney. He said he let Platt's son use his boat. Said he's friends with them."

"Hmm."

"He asked him to hang around for a minute. You want to ask anything else?"

"Nah. Let them go. But make sure he tells him to keep it quiet."

I pulled up Alice Wright's records. She was clean. Looking at the Hyundai, I realized I never requested owner-ship information on the Ford SUV and tapped on my phone. I never texted so much.

A sun-shower moved through the neighborhood. There wasn't enough rain to wet the street. As the steam rose off the asphalt, a text sounded.

The blue house was owned by an LLC called Acme Hold-ings. The generic-sounding company was located in Louisiana. I'd read about companies buying up single-family homes and renting them out. Maybe that's what this was. I Googled the name. A bunch of listings came up, but none appeared to be involved in real estate.

I went to the Louisiana Department of State to find out who was behind the limited liability company. What came up was another LLC named Acme Enterprises, with an address in Arizona.

The results from an Arizona company search raised a flag. The applicant, The Blue Water Group, was a corporation registered in Grand Cayman. The Caribbean island was known to house enterprises looking for privacy and favorable tax treatments.

Someone was looking to hide the ownership of this home. It was what a smart criminal would do. Something The Professor would do.

35

I hit the browser's back button. The Arizona company was formed last year on February 2. When I saw the date of the Louisiana company, I stood up. It was recognized by the state on February 1, the day before.

I Googled the Blue Water Group. There were plenty of results, but none were in Grand Cayman. Going to the Cayman Islands' government site proved useless. The chamber of commerce web page provided plenty of tourism-related businesses, but that was it.

Who was behind this interwoven set of companies? And why? I needed a name, someone to focus on.

We had something, but what was it? I missed talking things over with Derrick. What course of action was best? I wanted to send a team in, but if we did, the leaders, wherever they were, would scatter like rats.

Whether it was from staring at the screen or trying to figure the next step, I had a splitting headache. I closed my eyes to think. A second later I opened them. The video feeds needed monitoring.

Calling Connolly, I asked him to keep his eyes on the drone footage and headed to the parking lot.

———

ZIPPERING the sweater I kept in the Cherokee, I pushed through the glass doors of the medical examiner's office. The cool air felt like I was in Publix's produce department. At least they had an excuse to keep the veggies fresh. Here it didn't make sense; the bodies were refrigerated.

In the hallway just outside Bilotti's office, my phone pinged. It was a text from Connolly. I read it twice: "Platt is on the move."

"You going to come in, Frank?"

"Uh, yeah. Sorry." I stepped inside the office. "Give me a second, Doc."

I opened the app up and pulled up the video of Platt. He was in a boat navigating his way around the Ten Thousand Island area. There was no one on the boat with him, but there were three black bags in the cockpit.

The bags were large. Remembering that Everglades City was once the center of smuggling Columbian pot into Florida, I wondered if it was weed or hashish. Cocaine was a stretch. If it was coke, it would rank up there as the largest bust in Collier County history. If it was anything, I leaned toward weed.

There was a lot of pot being moved on the water, but most of it was headed into the Keys or the East Coast. Maybe these guys had revived an old pipeline. I extended my hand.

"Sorry. Someone we're watching is in motion."

"Someone connected to the ambush?"

"I wish I knew. This case has some of the thinnest evidence I've ever seen."

"Tough one."

"But we're making progress. I feel like we're on the cusp of something big."

"Well, that's encouraging."

"I'm not sure what to do, and you always have a good perspective."

"I don't know about that, but tell me what's going on."

"We've been watching a couple of locations in Everglades City. I had eyes on a home, when next door a FedEx truck then a UPS one made deliveries. When an Amazon van pulled up, it made me think of the dealers using courier companies to move their drugs, like Lopez did at Walgreens."

"Sounds risky, but I guess with the millions of packages going through the system, it's as safe as any other way."

"Sad but true. When the Amazon driver left the package by the door, a guy reached out and grabbed it. Seeing all those tattoos covering his arm made me look into the house. To cut to the chase, the house is owned by a series of companies ending in one based in the Cayman Islands."

"These operators are sophisticated."

"They are. I want to find out who's behind this. Going after the company seems the easiest way, am I right?"

"Maybe, but two things. First off, and I know this from a friend of mine with a place down there, a foreign person or entity setting up a company has to hire a local agent."

"Okay, so?"

"There are offices listing fifty to a hundred companies on the door of a single room and just one registered agent handling all of them."

"That's all right."

"I guarantee that if you start asking questions, they'd reach out and alert whoever it is behind it. Privacy is what makes the place attractive."

"Why would they want to encourage the type of behavior that requires such a level of privacy?"

He rubbed his fingers together. "Money, my friend."

"Greed, the ultimate motivator."

"Yes, and the other thing is, even if the agent told you, chances are that whoever is listed on the documentation is just a front man."

"I could lean on them."

"Of course, but you'd drive the true leader underground."

"I know. I'm just frustrated. I hear all the things you're saying. I want to force something. I feel like we're close to nailing this Professor thug."

"Professor?"

"That's what they call the top guy. Supposed to be supersmart."

"Hmm. I know you say they all make mistakes, but maybe there's a way to play off his intelligence."

"What do you mean?"

"Find a way to make him feel like he's outsmarted you. Make him confident to come out, take some risks. And when he does, you nail him."

"I have to know who he is, don't I?"

"Not necessarily. You may be able to flush him or her out if they feel confident enough."

"What you're saying sounds a lot like backing off. Waiting and watching."

"Maybe, but I'm not the detective here. Ultimately, it's your call on how to proceed with the investigation."

I left Bilotti's office and made a call as soon as I hit the parking lot.

"Connolly, did you observe any boats stopping by the campground and unloading."

"Just one, but it was a supply boat. They unloaded cases of water and food, stuff like that."

I didn't call him out, and my experience with drug interdiction was limited, but I had a feeling he missed something.

36

I watched Platt motor around a small island. If the bags were supplies for the campground, why would Platt be leaving with them?

Back in 1985, the feds had banned commercial fishing in Everglades National Park, and Everglades City's economy was decimated. With plenty of fishermen expert in navigating the swampy waters of the area, they went to work hauling bales of weed Columbian smugglers dropped in the area.

Most of the town ended up making money fishing for what they called square grouper. At its peak, they were collecting up to seventy-five tons a week. The activity pumped mounds of cash into the sleepy town, reviving its fortunes.

The party came to a halt when President Reagan launched the war on drugs. The feds ultimately arrested more than three hundred of the six hundred residents, confiscating hundreds of fishing boats in the process. Thirty-five years later, the town still hadn't regained its footing.

I wondered whether some sort of act two was underway. If so, was Platt a lone wolf or part of a larger enterprise?

Legalized marijuana for recreational use was spreading across the country, but Florida only permitted it for medicinal use. The state restricted the growers, outlets, and doctors allowed to be involved. I'd looked the other way when I encountered casual users, but this was too large not to check out.

Platt was making his way into Chokoloskee Bay. It looked like he was heading back home.

I made a call.

"Cisco, I need you to send a couple of cars out to Plantation Island. Platt is motoring his way back, and he may be carrying a large load of marijuana."

"Is he armed?"

"I don't know, but we have to assume he is."

"How many others?"

"He's alone on the boat, but there were at least two others at his house."

I gave him the address and told him I was watching him from above.

My heart began to race as Platt steered closer to Everglades City. I was waiting for him to turn into the inlet that led to Plantation Island but he bypassed it. Maybe he was going in on the other side of the town.

He passed the main entrance and continued north. I called Cisco and told him to hold off. Platt navigated around Bear Island. He sped up entering Lane Cove and headed toward West Pass Bay where a half a dozen boats were.

Platt piloted toward a small opening to Gate Bay. He cut the engine and drifted. I zoomed out. There was a larger boat in West Pass heading his way. As it closed in, Platt started his engine and squeezed through the inlet.

The two boats slowly converged. Both cut their engines.

They drifted toward each other and Platt tossed two bumpers over the side. Separated by a foot, Platt began swinging bags onto the larger boat. A shirtless man in a Yankees hat dragged the bags toward a cabin.

After a quick wave, they headed in opposite directions. I knew where to find Platt, so I kept the drone over the rendezvous vessel as it headed north. It motored into wide-open Fakahatchee Bay, speeding up as it headed into the Gulf of Mexico.

Marco Island was the first place I thought it might head to, but as Fort Myers came into my head as a possible destination, the fuel indicator began flashing red. There was only a two-hour window to safely land the drone.

There was no way I was going to end the surveillance this close to an arrest. The sheriff had a small fleet of boats I could access. We could intercept, but we'd give up the chance to nail the receivers.

The boat was at Marco Island's midpoint and made a right toward land. I called the sheriff's substation and alerted them. The water was crowded with fishermen and recreational boaters. I kept an eye on them, trying to determine which of the many docking places the pot was headed for.

A large rubber raft with an outboard motor zigged and zagged its way toward the contraband carrier, pulling alongside. The plastic bags were handed off, and the raft sped toward the island. It was destined for the Marco Island Marina.

The app began beeping, and a stream of red ran across the top. The drone's fuel reserve had kicked in. It was critically low. I resisted the urge to panic, keeping my eyes on the raft until three cars crossed Jolly West Bridge.

Marco Island Executive Airport was not on the island but

just east of Hammock Bay. It would be a perfect place to land it. I called Connolly and told him to take over the landing. Putting the phone away, I realized something important.

I dug my phone out.

"Cisco, tell Marco to back off. I don't want a scene at the dock. Have them follow at a safe distance. If a handoff is made, I want details, but I don't want anyone stopped."

"Stand down?"

"Yes, back away from the marina. Let the rafter go. We need to keep watching before we move in on anybody. I don't want anyone getting spooked at this point."

"You got it. I'll tell them to lay off. What about that guy Platt, on Plantation Island?"

"Leave him alone. He's heading in. I want to watch him. This looks like a weed pipeline, and I don't think these guys are mixed up in the ambush. It looks like we got lucky running into it with the surveillance we're doing."

"Maybe the Chinese got it right with all the cameras they got over there."

"No way, man. The way we do it here, it may not be perfect, but at least you have to have a reason to watch someone."

"What's to stop anyone from using a drone? Or a satellite, like they do in the military?"

It was a good question. Technology was creating situations that could turn ugly. The Chinese were watching their people to keep them in line. It wasn't pretty, but at least the citizens knew about it.

With drones flying out of view and the growing use of satellites outfitted with powerful cameras, you'd be afraid to pick your nose in public. People shared too much information willingly, which we knew was dangerous. The likelihood it was going to go way past that scared me. I had doubts society would muster the necessary pushback.

Setting the larger picture aside, I devised a plan that relied on drones. The first order of business was identifying who owned the boat Platt handed the goods off to and the raft.

37

―――――

We'd retrieved a couple of plastic bags from the garbage picked up at Platt's house. They tested positive for weed. I called the sheriff and asked to see him.

Chester was looking in the mirror hanging in his closet when I was shown into his office. Adjusting his tie, he said, "Sit down. I'll be right with you. I splashed coffee on my shirt and have a civilian outreach event in Golden Gate in an hour."

"No problem, sir."

He ran a finger around his collar and sat. "Nice work uncovering the marijuana pipeline. We haven't seen anything like that in decades."

"It appears to be a serious smuggling operation."

"That's why you want to work it further?"

"Yes, I want to make sure they're out of business for another thirty years."

"It's going to take time neither of us has. It'd be a heck of a win for the department if we arrest these guys. I can see the pictures with all the marijuana stacked up."

"I'd appreciate a little patience. I'll develop further—"

"I think it may be better to turn this over to Kirby's team. They have the manpower to take it off your plate. That way, you can concentrate on tracking down the ambushers."

"I understand and appreciate the offer, but there looks to be a connection between the two."

It was a borderline lie. There was almost no chance of an alliance, but I'd uncovered the pipeline and I wanted credit for it. I told myself it was necessary to have something in the win column if I wasn't able to bring in those responsible for the ambush. There was some truth to that, but after what the department put me through, I wanted to show them just how good I was.

"That would seem to stretch you too far. If Detective Dickson was around, it'd be another story."

"I understand, sir, but if you can spare me Connolly and two more drones, I won't need any help."

"You're working too many leads, following too many people. It's impossible to cover it all."

"It's a department effort, sir. I feel strongly about being the lead on this. It's sensitive, and I want to direct the investigation."

"I'm not convinced that's the correct course of action. It's best if we use the manpower we have and wrap it up as soon as possible."

"Broadening the scope of people involved may compromise the investigation."

Chester put his hands on the table. "What are you getting at?"

"It's nothing definitive, sir. But there are huge amounts of money at stake here, and I wouldn't want a leak to alert them when we're so close."

He leaned across the desk. "Are you insinuating some

level of cooperation from someone inside this department? If so, I'd suggest you inform me right now."

"It's nothing concrete, sir."

"Out with it."

"I'd rather not speak ill of anyone who's taken the oath, sir. But if there's something there, I'll know shortly."

Chester fell back in his chair. "If there's anything, you bring it to me immediately. Is that understood?"

"Of course, sir."

"I'm going to allow you to continue. You'll get Connolly and the drones, but the clock is ticking."

WE HAD JUST GOTTEN SHOWN to a table at First Watch. I wasn't a big fan of going out to breakfast, but Jessie loved it. I knew it was only a matter of a couple of years before friends would replace me, and thus we had begun to make it a Saturday morning ritual.

She didn't even need to look at the menu. "I'm having the Florida French Toast. It's the bestest! What are you having, Dad?"

I wanted to have a stack of pancakes, but Mary Ann had been on me about eating healthier. I'd put on five pounds from the inactivity connected to watching drone footage.

"I think I'm going to get the Super Foods Bowl."

"You're not having a stack of pancakes?"

My phone vibrated. "Mom said this is better for me." I pulled out my cell. "I have to get this. Put our order in."

Answering the call, I stepped outside. The traffic on Tamiami Trail was backed up. Looking through the window, I kept my eyes on Jessie and asked, "What's going on?"

"Nothing came up on the hull numbers."

I knew the answer but still asked, "How in God's name can that be?"

"They must have put something bogus on the boat. The numbers don't match anything."

"Can you get the lab to make some pictures of the craft? We'll circulate them around marinas, see if anyone can ID it or who was piloting it."

"Sure. I'll grab the best section of the video to make stills out of."

"All right. Talk to you later."

Even the damn potheads were taking every precaution they could, I thought, and headed back inside.

"Sorry, honey. It was work."

"But it's Saturday. You're supposed to be off."

I couldn't take time off if I was going to catch such a clever group of criminals. "I know, but the bad guys don't take any days off."

"That's funny, Dad, criminals taking a vacation."

I wished they did. "Oh, here comes our food."

The server delivered our breakfast. As I dug into my bowl, I noticed a card on the table with nutritional information. What I'd ordered was a thousand calories. How could they call it a healthy dish? It tasted good but was misleading.

Stabbing a strawberry, the idea that the marijuana pipeline could be some kind of diversion crept into my thoughts. It was as far-out an idea as I'd had, but with the lengths these guys went to, I couldn't discount it.

38

I avoided going out to the driveway for the Sunday paper. Instead, I sipped my coffee, alternating between sifting through my email and watching the Jasmine Street house.

Yesterday had been a busy day for arrests. Collier County averaged ten arrests a day, but the list I skimmed looked twice as long. Saturdays were always a wild card, especially with DUIs.

The name Rosario sounded familiar, and in his mug shot I could make out a neck tattoo. I clicked through for details. He'd been arrested under the public nuisance ordinance.

I pulled up his record, but it only had an old DUI. Staring at his face, I caught movement in my peripheral vision. A white Mustang was pulling up the driveway of the Jasmine home.

An older, skinny male got out. He was holding a gym bag. Looking both ways, he headed to the door. Before he knocked, it opened. The thin man stepped in.

What was in the bag? A change of clothes? Or was it drugs or money from the night's drug sales? Zooming in on the Mustang's plate, the man came back out of the house. He no longer had the bag.

I jotted down the plate number as he got in the car. He turned onto Jasmine Street, and a blue pickup truck came down the road. They slowed passing each other and exchanged words.

As the Mustang left the camera's coverage, the pickup turned into the driveway. This time the driver had a huge bald spot. He was holding a cigarette with one hand and a back-pack with the other.

Baldy was let into the house and reappeared minutes later. It was another drop. I was sure the bags contained drugs or money. Now I had something to follow. I hoped it was cash, because if it were drugs, it would only lead me to street dealers.

Both runners were in their late fifties or sixties. The use of older bagmen made me think it was money. They were less likely to raise suspicion, and, chances were, they wouldn't run with the dough.

At times, dealers used kids to move drugs around, knowing the courts would be gentler on minors engaged in trafficking. Older adults knew being caught with large amounts of drugs would keep them from seeing the sun for a long time.

Mary Ann came into the kitchen in her bathing suit. "I'm going to do my laps."

"Go for it."

"When Jessie gets up, make her something to eat."

"You got it." I watched her walk onto the lanai. All the exercising she was doing, especially the swimming, was help-ing. I was thankful she decided to push back on MS instead of adopting a "poor me" attitude. She was tough, sometimes too much so.

I GOT UP AND STRETCHED. It was half past noon. There had been no activity at the Jasmine house since the morning drops. Mary Ann stuck her head into the family room.

"You going to get ready?"

"What time we supposed to be there?"

"Carolyn said around one."

A neighbor was having a barbecue for the original home-owners in the community. Every year she held what she called a Settler's Party. It was fun seeing people who had moved out and catch up with everyone, but I wanted to phone this one in.

"Why so early?"

She gave me the kind of look that shut down the idea to try and get out of going. "Because the kids have school tomorrow."

"All right. Shorts okay?"

"Sure, but no flip-flops."

I put the laptop on the vanity and brushed my teeth. Taking a swig of Listerine, I noticed a car pulling into the Jasmine Street driveway. It was a white Honda. A gray-haired woman in a flowery sundress got out. Across her body she wore a small, white pocketbook.

It looked like a social visit. The door cracked open as her foot hit the first step. She disappeared inside. I picked up the laptop and carried it into the kitchen.

"What are you watching, Dad?"

"A house we have under surveillance."

"It's Sunday. Can't somebody else do it?"

"Your father doesn't trust anyone else."

"That's not true. This is a special case; we think it involves the people who shot Uncle Derrick."

"It's sure taking a long time to get them."

"Yes, but sometimes, to do it right, we need to take our time and build a case."

Mary Ann opened the refrigerator and took a platter out. "Okay, let's go. Frank, grab a bottle of wine. Carolyn likes white."

I went into the closet and pulled a bottle of Sauvignon Blanc out of the rack. "You have a bag for this?"

"In the drawer by the pantry."

I slipped the bottle in and took a last look at the drone footage. The woman was coming out of the house. She was carrying a satchel. The trunk to her car opened and she put the bag in. Looking both ways, she got in the car and backed out of the driveway.

"Frank! Let's go."

I handed the wine to Jessie. "I'll meet you over there. This could be it."

"All right, but you better make an appearance."

Cell phone to my ear, I said, "I will. Have a good time."

"Connolly, we've got something. A white Honda, with a female driver, is leaving the Jasmine house. I think she's moving money."

"What do you want me to do?"

"I'm going to follow her, but I want to keep eyes on the house. Move a drone over, and let me know if there's any activity."

"You got it."

Sitting behind the desk in my home office, I opened another tab, taking me to the DMV portal. The Honda belonged to Alice Pastiche of Cape Coral. The name reminded me of *The Alice Network*, a book about the French Resistance during the German occupation of France.

This Alice, a sixty-two-year-old with clear blue eyes, was

no hero. She had a record. Though her last arrest was fifteen years ago in Jacksonville, it was drug related. She was caught in possession of twenty-three grams of cocaine. Anything over ten grams was considered trafficking, and she served three years for the offense.

I increased the height the drone was flying at as I followed Alice out of Everglades City.

39

———

Alice drove along Route 29, staying well under the speed limit. The road was empty. I wished she'd step on it and get to where she was going. Approaching the intersection with Route 41, I thought she might continue straight to Route 75, but she turned and headed toward Naples.

She continued driving west as I tried to guess where a rendezvous might take place. I lost my bet that is was somewhere in East Naples when she slowed down, turning left onto San Marco Road.

It was the alternative way to get to Marco Island. It didn't make sense. If that's where she was going, it was faster to go by boat. Platt's pot shipment had also landed on Marco. Was there anything to the coincidence? Was the island home to more than tourists?

Alice weaved her way onto the island. The traffic at the intersection of San Marco and Barfield Drive was backed up to the Marco Veterinary Hospital. She made a right onto Barfield, and the going was slow as she circled the island.

She was headed in the direction of the Marco Island Marina, the same one used by the Platt associate. I was beginning to think maybe I hadn't fibbed to the sheriff after all. As Alice approached North Collier Boulevard, I was sure she was going to make a right toward the docks.

Instead, she turned left and pulled into the parking lot for the SpeakEasy, a Prohibition-inspired waterfront restaurant. I'd taken Mary Ann there when we were dating. It was a fun place with great views, and the prices were something a cop could afford.

I watched her walk into the establishment. She was carrying the bag. It was going to be a handoff. My eyes were glued to the screen. The restaurant had a nice deck, but she didn't seem to be on it.

Where was she? And who was she meeting? The thought to send in an undercover cop crossed my mind, but I was afraid of someone blowing it. Using a drone had some major advantages, but I needed to get inside and couldn't.

A half hour passed. Maybe she was getting lunch and didn't want to leave the cash unattended. It was plausible. The thought she was enjoying a juicy Roaring Twenties burger while my eyes bled pissed me off.

I carried the laptop into the kitchen and opened the fridge, grabbing a Tupperware with leftovers. Keeping my eyes on the screen, I pulled open a drawer and fished out a fork.

The first forkful of pasta with cauliflower was in my mouth when Alice came out of the SpeakEasy. Empty-handed. She put sunglasses on and went to her car. I searched the video feed for someone with the satchel she'd brought in.

No one else came out the front. I searched the strip of docking that lined both sides of the restaurant's deck. A man in shorts and a T-shirt was stepping onto a boat. He had the bag.

I watched him cast off, slowly pulling away from the dock. The boat passed under an overpass and entered Factory

Bay. The color of the water changed as he headed toward the Gulf of Mexico. Once in open water, he went north, hugging the coastline.

As he skirted Keewaydin Island, I recalled one of the first homicide cases I'd investigated in Collier. A woman from one of the wealthiest families in town had been found dead on their private compound on the island. The brutal crime scene on the serene island flashed through my mind as the boat turned into Gordon Pass.

Was the leader of a drug gang living in the exclusive area known as Port Royal? The gossipy social scene would require a legitimate cover or he'd stick out.

Rows of fancy homes with matching boats were laid out on small peninsulas. I wondered what palace he was going to, but he didn't turn into the ritzy area. He continued north, passing another expensive area called Aqualane Shores. The roofs of the homes were meandering and massive.

The water darkened as he motored past Crayton Cove. It looked like he was destined for the Naples City Dock, which was thick with all kinds of crafts. He slowed down approaching the large marina but didn't turn into a slip. He edged around the docking and proceeded toward The Boathouse on Naples Bay.

Sporting a hundred-foot-long dock, the green Tiki-roofed restaurant was a favorite of boaters and tourists. The wait for your food could be long, but with a great view and bar, most visitors didn't seem to mind.

He threw a bumper over the side and tied up behind a raft that ferried people to sailboats. It was almost three o'clock, but you'd never know it by the eatery's packed deck. I watched him swap his T-shirt for a button-down. He grabbed the bag, hopped on the deck, and went inside.

I flew the drone farther away but lower, trying to get a

view of the umbrella-forested deck. It was impossible to get a fix whether he was on the deck or not. A couple left the restaurant, but neither were carrying bags.

My pee alarm sounded, and I carried the laptop into the bathroom. Unzipping, I saw him. Not the boater but a man wearing a straw fedora and sunglasses exit the restaurant. It was him. He had the satchel of cash.

The suspect was about five foot ten and fit. He walked leisurely toward the parking lot. I surveyed the cars, guessing his was going to be white and nondescript.

He grabbed the handle of a white Mercedes SUV. I considered myself right; in Naples, Benzes were a dime a dozen. I jotted down the plate number and plugged it into the DMV portal. It was registered to Acme Enterprises. We didn't have a name, but the connection meant we were close.

Mystery Man drove under the speed limit, no small feat given the twenty to twenty-five-mile-per-hour limits in the area. He crossed over Fifth Avenue and made his way onto Route 41, heading north.

He made a left onto Neapolitan Way, in the direction of Venetian Village, into an area known as Park Shore. He made a right onto Crayton Road. When he made a left onto Devil's Lane, pulling into the second home, I snickered. How appropriate.

40

THE COUNTY TAX RECORDS LISTED ACME ENTERPRISES AS THE owner of 2 Devil's Lane. We needed to identify the man living there. The utilities were paid for by the company as well. Asking questions in the neighborhood would raise alarms.

We had watched the house for two days, and except a shapely woman visitor, there were no other visitors and Mystery Man never left. I picked up the phone.

"Connolly, I'm getting itchy. We need to find out who the hell this guy is."

"He's gotta leave the house sometime."

"I was thinking about setting up a bogus DUI blockade on Forty-One or Crayton Road."

"That's a damn good idea. I love it. I say we do it."

"We have to wait until he establishes some kind of routine, otherwise it could backfire."

"Maybe send someone to the house, like to register to vote or something, maybe a kid's charity drive."

"He's too cautious to give up any information. He could make it up."

"Can we check his mail? He's gotta have health insurance or something he can't fake."

"You know what? Let's grab some of his garbage and test it for DNA."

"Oh, I like that. I'll check to see when the next collection is."

WHEN THE LAB ran the DNA against the databases, we came up empty. The Professor had no record. Even the search for a familial connection didn't turn up any links to explore. It was time to go big.

I had the perfect idea. It was bold and needed the sheriff to sign off on it. There was not a doubt in my mind that he'd push back against it. As I walked into his office, my confidence began to wane.

"Have a seat, Frank."

"Thanks, sir."

"I don't have much time. What did you want to see me about?"

"I think we've got the boss running the drug ring."

"Good. Bring him in."

"We're still unclear about exactly who he is and his involvement in the ambush. Lopez said he was, but he was assassinated and can't testify."

"What is your plan, then?"

"I want to grab the mule who delivered the money to him."

"But that'll scare him off."

"Not the way I want to do it."

Chester beckoned with his hand.

"We've been watching him. He's got a lady friend he

visits out on Capri Island. They hang out at the Island Gypsy Bar. What I want to do is grab him on the way back. At night, on Route Nine Fifty-Two."

"How you going to keep the boss from finding out?"

"We fake an accident. We dump his car in the water, make it look like he drove off the road and drowned."

"This is not the movies, Luca."

"I'm serious, sir. I know I can make it work. I just need you to sign off. We'll close down the road, have the press run a story or two."

"Let's say it works. How can you be sure he'll talk?"

"He's not going to have a choice. We protect him if he agrees to testify, but if he doesn't and we let him go, I'm sure we'll find his body in a couple of days."

"I understand the low regard for life that this gang has, but faking a death? Isn't there another way?"

"Not that I see, sir. We've had three executions, that we're aware of, and an attack on our department. Anyone on the inside knows if they talk, they're dead."

"Can't we just bring the mule in and offer him immunity?"

"That'll cause him to run. We know he's got a connection with the Cayman Islands and probably has enough money down there to disappear."

"We have an extradition agreement with them. It's covered in our treaty with Great Britain."

"I understand, sir, but I'm sure he can buy off someone or use the Caymans to jump off and go somewhere we can't touch him."

"I'd like you to brainstorm some more. Find another alternative. It's just too risky, and we'd need the press's cooperation."

"Not exactly, sir. The way I see it, we grab him, drive the

car into the water, and get a diver and the medical examiner out there. We notify the press after the body is supposedly in the ME van."

"How are you going to keep anybody from seeing what's being staged?"

"We close down the road."

"Look for another way." He stood. "I've got to go."

I trudged down the stairs to my office. Connolly was sitting behind Derrick's desk.

"What are you doing?"

"What do you mean? I'm watching the drone footage."

"Do me a favor, will you? Don't sit in my partner's chair."

"What?"

"You heard me."

He turned the laptop to the front side of the desk. "Chester said no, didn't he?"

I nodded as he sat in a guest chair. "Now what?"

"I got no damn idea. We have to hope something breaks, and fast, or I'm going to go crazy."

"Speaking of crazy. Simmons just told me some kid hopped the sidewalk and crashed into a bunch of people eating outside."

"Where was this?"

"Fifth Avenue."

"How the hell did that happen?"

"Looks like the kid overdosed. They had to hit her with Naloxone to revive her."

"Jesus. Anybody else hurt?"

"Nothing too serious from what he said."

"I'll be right back."

The sheriff had his jacket on and was talking to a prosecutor outside his office. I raised a finger. He frowned and shook his head. When he headed for the elevator, I stepped in.

"I don't have time, Luca."

"I just wanted to make sure you knew that the incident on Fifth was drug-related. The crap this gang is pushing is going to destroy everything we've worked for if we don't stamp it out."

The doors began to open. "We don't know it's related at this point."

I followed him into the elevator. "I know it is, and it's our duty to stop it. We don't have time. This is going to disrupt tourism and give the town a black eye."

He hesitated before stepping out.

"I know you believe my plan isn't the best, but as long as we're careful, and we will be, we can put these bastards out of business."

His driver was waiting by the door to the parking lot. He nodded and turned to me, lowering his voice.

"I'll approve this, but if you embarrass this department, there'll be consequences. Do I make myself clear?"

"Yes, sir. I understand. You can count on me."

The problem was there were going to be too many people involved. It not only had to go flawlessly, everyone had to keep their mouths shut.

41

———

There wasn't a cloud in the sky as we approached the turnoff to Capri Island. I turned up the AC, saying, "Almost there, Doc. I really appreciate you taking the ride with me. This has to be believable."

"Anytime, Frank."

Pointing to the water on both sides of the road, I said, "So along here is where I'm figuring we can stage it."

"Where is the deepest water?"

I slowed down, pointing to the left. "According to the nautical map, it's the Tarpon Bay side."

"Pull over."

The sun beat on my back as we walked along the road. Bilotti said, "The water along here isn't deep enough to submerge a vehicle. He'd have to be traveling so fast that the momentum would carry the car farther out. With the brush, I just don't see it."

"Are you sure?"

"I'm afraid so. You mentioned this person would be coming from a bar, so he'd probably have been drinking."

"Yeah, that's right."

"If you could get the car to flip onto its roof. You could use the alcohol factor to your advantage. Alcohol disorients and slows reaction times. It's the reason why half of drownings involve drinking."

"Fifty percent? I didn't realize that."

"Some studies indicate even higher rates of causation, up to seventy percent."

"I hope there aren't many wine drinkers in the group."

He smiled. "Safe to say, I've never been in the pool with a glass of Bordeaux. A chilled Chablis? Maybe."

We kept walking west. "Red wine and heat don't mix."

"A cold Chablis is nice in the afternoon by the pool."

"Invite me over."

"You got it. Look, the water is closer to the road up ahead. And by the color, it's deeper as well."

"Could be the spot. Only problem is how to get the car on its back."

"If you're in control of the scene, it doesn't need to be. Have the department tow truck flip it over. I bet from here they can slide it far enough to fill it with water."

"Good idea, Doc. You know, it's not just for the wine that I keep you around."

THERE WERE enough people and equipment to stage a small theater company. At the briefing, the sheriff warned everyone that secrecy was paramount and promised if there was a leak, he was going to chase it down and hold those accountable.

Though I welcomed it, it wasn't for me; it was to protect him and the department. He'd be the one roasted by the press if this scheme slipped out.

However, if we were able to take down the drug ring,

he'd be the one leaking, especially around a reelection campaign. It would play in his favor. He'd be able to parade around saying that he was prepared to do anything to keep our county safe.

I took up a position in the Capri Paddlecraft Park, knowing I couldn't look that far out. Chances were that by the time his term was up, I'd be long gone. The job was changing me.

The truth was I was letting it. My obsessive nature was at fault. I was unable to strike the right balance, and I didn't want to jeopardize my family by hanging around too long.

It was just past midnight. We had two men undercover, one in the Island Gypsy Bar and another waiting in the parking lot. Once Terry Jackson left, the patrol cars parked next to me would swing into action. Jackson usually left the bar around one.

The coffee in my thermos was still hot. Though the adrenaline was building, I needed the boost. I took a sip thinking we had less than an hour before conducting what was essentially a legal kidnapping. It was like a war movie where we catch someone on the other side to get information.

Only in this case, instead of beating the captured to extract what we wanted, we'd dangle a fresh start, knowing it wasn't the chance at a new beginning but the ability to stay alive that would turn Jackson.

The radio crackled with confirmation that a pair of tow trucks had pulled into Hammock Bay. They were ten minutes away. I took another sip and the radio sounded again. It was Tim Yale sitting in the bar's parking lot.

"Our boy just exited."

I grabbed the handset. "Copy that."

"The subject is in his car, heading in your direction."

"Copy. We're in motion."

Both patrol cars left the lot. I needed to hang back for deniability. Shifting in my seat, I stared out the windshield into the blackness, considering the moonless night a godly omen.

Leaning forward, I listened to the radio chatter. They had stopped Jackson. Two minutes later, Yale said, "Subject secured and roadblocks in place."

"I'm on my way. Tows, we have a car in the water and need assistance."

Pulling onto Route 952, I saw the patrol car's strobe lights. My heart pounded as I approached the eastern blockage. I radioed and he backed up, getting back in place as I passed.

Jackson's beige Buick was parked on a grassy shoulder. Yale was outside his car talking to Jackson, who was cuffed and had his head down. Approaching, I surveyed the bay. It was empty. In the distance, I could see the lights from the patrol car at the west end of the road.

"Any trouble?"

Yale said, "Went off without a hitch. Both he and the car are clean."

I went over to the vehicle and checked the interior and trunk.

"Mr. Jackson, I'm Detective Luca."

He raised his head but said nothing.

"You have anything of value in your vehicle?"

Jackson remained silent.

"If you have something you want, this is your last chance to get it." I pointed to a set of lights flashing. "That's a tow truck. You're never going to see your car again, and it's not because you're being arrested."

He looked up for the first time, and I said, "If you want something, tell me. If not, you're coming with me."

Jackson didn't move.

I pulled Yale aside. "Take that case in the back seat and get it to my office."

"Whatever you say."

I took Jackson by the arm and locked him in the back seat of the cruiser I was driving.

"Yale, put it over the radio as soon as Bilotti gets here. Keep the press at a distance. Let them seem the body bag but nothing more."

"Will do."

"And don't forget to send me some pictures."

I slipped into the front seat as a tow truck lumbered around the blockade. The first part of the plan was working.

42

———————

Jackson had not said a word. He was sitting in an interrogation room, and I was sitting on the bowl trying to coax out a leak. The bladder my doctors fashioned out of my intestines was giving me a hard time.

Not relieving myself on a regular basis always caused the improvised bladder to freeze up. The doctors warned me that the new bladder needed to be trained and a routine maintained, but my job always stepped in the way.

Ten minutes of massaging my abdomen and a trickle finally started. It ebbed and flowed, but even though the nerves were dead, I sensed relief as a text chimed in.

Boyle had sent pictures. Hollywood couldn't have put on a better production. In the first one, only the wheels and undercarriage of Jackson's car was visible as it sat in the bay. Two others had the vehicle on its roof, water pouring out as it was dragged out of the cove.

Dr. Bilotti was in another photo. He was pointing toward a spot on the road as a gurney, with a body bag on it, was rolled to the medical examiner's van.

What was even better was him sharing the images with

WINK News. These would be a helpful sign of the power we had over Jackson's fate. He was closemouthed but had not asked to see a lawyer.

Washing up, I smiled at my image. As tired as I was of the bullshit working for the sheriff, what was coming up was the fun part of the job.

I shifted the can of Coke and Mars bar I'd gotten in the cafeteria to one hand and opened the door.

"These are for you."

Jackson took the can and popped the top. Closing his bloodshot eyes, he took a long guzzle. He put the Coke down and reached for the candy. As he took a bite, I said, "We know you're part of a gang dealing in Schedule One drugs. I don't have to tell you; I'm sure you know plenty of people serving long prison terms from it."

"And you got some deal for me, right?"

"That's true, and it happens to be your only way out."

He put the rest of the bar in his mouth and began tearing the wrapper into tiny pieces as he chewed.

"Tell me who's running this thing, and we'll protect you. You'll go in a witness protection program, and we look the other way regarding your involvement. All you have to do is testify against him, and we'll help you get a fresh start."

He smiled and shook his head. "You think I'd do something like that? I'd end up dead."

"Let me show you something." I showed him my phone. "You recognize the car?"

"What the fuck did you do to my car? My favorite cue stick was in there."

I stepped outside the room, grabbed the case from his car and came back. Handing the pool stick to him, I said, "Here you go."

He opened it and I said, "Look here." I swiped my phone, pointing to the body bag.

"Who's that?"

"You."

"Me? Get the fuck outta here."

"You said you wouldn't help us because you'd be assassinated. You don't have to worry; we took care of that."

Jackson crossed his arms.

I sat on the corner of the table. "Look, you have two choices. If you go back, you'll be executed, just like Arturo Lopez was. You won't even last a day. You know how The Professor operates."

"I'd rather go to prison than run my mouth."

I laughed. "You think you'd be safe there? Not after I spread the word you talked."

He cursed me under his breath, and I said, "Come on, Terry. You don't have a family. We can move your girl if you want—"

"No fucking way with her, man."

"So, what do you say?"

"I want me a lawyer."

"No problem. You're making the right decision."

"Got no damn choice."

"It's going to work out good for you. We'll take care good care of you. Say, what do you want to eat? A steak?"

"Yeah, sounds good. Make it a rib eye and a baked potato."

"You got it. Say, what's The Professor's real name?"

"Julio Castro."

I HAD GOTTEN home at 4 a.m. and set the alarm for eight thirty. The public defender's office was sending over an attorney at ten. I wasn't going to leave any time for Jackson to have a change of heart.

I stumbled out of bed and put a pod of coffee in the machine. Reaching for the remote, I saw Mary Ann in the pool. I flicked the TV to the news. An annoying lawyer commercial came on, and I shifted my attention outside.

Mary Ann did one of those underwater change of direction she'd been practicing. With all the swimming she was doing, she was morphing into a fish. I grabbed the milk, remembering the time last week she had me try it. I got so much water up my nose that I choked.

The weather gal droned on about the possibility of rain. She was talking about sometime during the week. Then it was on to the traffic. It was moving slow on Route 75 because of an expansion project by Corkscrew Road.

I put my coffee down when they mentioned the deadly accident on Capri Island. It was perfect. Pictures of the car and Jackson's DMV photo splashed across the screen.

It gave me a bigger boost of energy than the java had. I was regretting only having a subscription for the Sunday edition of the *Naples Daily News*. I went online but couldn't find anything on the staged death.

I called Connolly. "Morning, Frank. Late night, huh?"

"Yeah, but it was worth it. Came off like pros. Anything to report?"

"No. There's been no activity on Devil's Lane or Everglades."

"Okay. You get the *Daily News*?"

"Yeah, why?"

"They have anything on last night?"

"Oh yeah, right on the front page."

"Nice. All right, keep your eyes open. I'll talk to you later."

Mary Ann was drying off. I stepped onto the lanai.

"You got in so late."

"I know, but it was worth it. We're so close I can taste it."

"I really hope so."

"I know I've been a little obsessed, but once this is over, I think I'm getting out."

"One thing at a time."

"I know. Love you; see you later."

"Call me; let me know what's going on."

43

———

WE HAD AN IMMUNITY AND PROTECTION AGREEMENT IN PLACE for Jackson. It covered everything, including conspiracy to murder but not the act of killing. As long as he gave us the information he claimed to know, I could live with letting him off the hook.

My goal was to bring down Julio Castro, and it was time to get inside the organization he ran. I walked into the interview room and slid two documents across the table.

"We're all set. Here's the agreement, signed by the twentieth district circuit office of the state attorney. There's an executed copy for you."

Thomas Krieger, the public defender assigned to Jackson, picked the papers up. As he reviewed them, his client's shoulders sagged. I said, "You want anything else to drink?"

"Nah."

"We're working on a nicer safe house for you."

He shrugged. I wanted to kick this off and said, "Counselor, nothing has changed. Can we get started?"

"Yes." He turned to Jackson and said, "Everything is in order."

"You sure?"

"Yes. You're safe from prosecution and will receive protection and a new identity if you're honest in revealing what you know."

I clicked on the video recorder and recited the formalities.

"How did you meet Julio Castro?"

"A friend of mine, I grew up with him; he was a good guy, but, you know, from the time he was little, he was selling shit."

"Drugs?"

"Yeah."

"He introduced you to Mr. Castro?"

"No. He never even met him. I was looking to make some money, you know, and one of the guys I played pool a lot with, he was connected to some of the Mexicans. He could play his ass off, but he'd make all kinds of crazy bets that made no sense. I was always good with math, you know, and I used to tell him not to give ten to one odds and shit but he—"

"Get back to the Castro connection."

"So, you see, this friend, he had a tight mouth. Most people knew he was involved but not more than that."

"What's his name?"

"Oh, come on, man. I can't drop it on him. You said this was about Castro—"

A pool-playing dealer who liked to gamble wouldn't be tough to hunt down. "All right, let's stick with Castro. This friend of yours did what?"

"Like I said, I knew someone who could get them smack, and next thing I know, this guy Sammy, he came up to me. He felt me out and shit, wanted to see if it was legit. So, I got a sample, and they were interested."

"You bought from your pool-playing buddy and sold it to

Sammy?"

"No, I never seen Sammy again. And I never carry drugs; it's too dangerous."

I almost laughed at the sanctimonious comment. "How does this get you to Mr. Castro?"

"It was the way I did things, you know. I was, like, careful. They didn't know I was scared shit, you know. When they had to pay, I made them meet me out in the bay, only one guy in the boat, that kind of thing."

"Didn't they suspect that you'd try to steal the first time?"

"No, it's the way they did things, you know. And they tried to get over on me on the first deal."

"How so?"

"The briefcase they handed over was short. They popped it open and closed it quickly. I saw there were two rows of six bundles. They were supposed to pay a hundred and thirty K. But there was only one twenty. I called 'em out and made them make a call before they left, so I knew I'd get the other money or I wouldn't make a dime."

"Tell me about Castro."

"We did, I don't know, ten deals, and on each one I changed the handoffs. You know, they were sending the same guy, and I told them if they did, I wasn't going to go through with it. Next thing I know, I'm told to go out fishing in Hammock Bay, and who shows up is Julio."

"Castro?"

"Yes."

"Who was with him?"

"Nobody. Just him."

"What did he want?"

"He wanted to talk. Asked me a bunch of questions, if I had a wife and whatnot. Said he heard I was a math whiz or something. He was nice, quiet, but I was nervous, you know."

"You didn't discuss any business?"

"No. He talked about fishing with his father and that was it. He said he liked the way I ran my end, you know, and he left."

"What happened next?"

"A week went by, and one of his guys came in the pool hall, said to go to breakfast at Blueberry at nine the next morning. I was like, nine?"

"Castro was there?"

"No, man, it was Arturo."

"Lopez?"

"Yeah. He told me to get up to Venice, to the Zebra Lounge for happy hour. That's where Castro was, sipping a seltzer. You know, he don't drink or nothing."

"What did you talk about?"

"We went for a walk; he asked how I'd put distance between someone like him and the drugs and money. I told him, you should always change things up, you know, routine shit is the pits. He agreed. He said you could never be too careful, and I said he was right, but that it was just as important to not be too comfortable, 'cause that's when you start cutting corners. Man, he ate that up, and next thing you know, I'm setting up the drops and gathering the cash."

"You told him to use the courier companies?"

"No, that was all him, and you gotta hand it to him, it was slick."

Jackson told me how Castro had just started getting fentanyl from China using third-party sellers on eBay and Amazon. I couldn't believe my ears. We could get warrants and enough evidence to put his ass away for the drugs, but I wanted him for the ambush. I was about to steer it that way when Jackson said he had to take a leak.

44

AFTER THE POTTY BREAK, HE SAID HE WAS HUNGRY. WE went to the cafeteria. Jackson walked back and forth, looking over the options several times.

I said, "Hate to tell you, the choices aren't going to change. They make a decent sandwich."

We were finally back in the interview room. Jackson unwrapped a roast beef sandwich. It looked good. He took a bite and I said, "You mentioned Arturo Lopez earlier. Did Castro assassinate him?"

Jackson shrugged.

"You have to tell me. As long as you weren't the trigger-man, you have nothing to worry about."

He swallowed. "I could never do something like that."

"How did it go down?"

"Castro was getting crazy paranoid, you know? If he felt something was off, you was in trouble. When Arturo got picked up, he said that he had to go. I was like, Arturo is not gonna talk, boss, but he said, you can never be too careful. Make sure he doesn't talk."

In between bites, Jackson said that he gave the order to someone else, who arranged to hire the hitman.

That was conspiracy to murder. "Who killed him?"

"I don't know. Nobody knew. I don't know for sure, but one of the guys told me that they used to put five pieces of paper with a green mark and just one with a red one in a bag. Nobody knew who got what, but the guy with the red, he had to do it."

"Lopez told us that The Professor was the one behind the ambush of my partner at the trailer off Santa Barbara Boulevard."

He shook his head. "I told him it was a mistake, but Castro, when he heard someone was talking to the cops, he went, like, you know, he never lost his cool, never got in your face or anything, so you never knew what he was thinking. But when he heard Ayala was going to open his mouth, man, he lost it."

"How did he find out?"

He balled up the sandwich wrapping. "You kidding? The boss would hand over a stack of cash to anyone who brought him information on anyone in the group. If someone got a new ride, he knew about it before the dude left the dealership. If someone cut a corner, he'd go a month without getting paid, if he was lucky."

He shook his head. "Oh, man, this one time, Pedro was supposed to leave Marco Island on one of the boats we got. He was to go to the Everglades and switch to another boat for a drop in Naples Bay. But he got lazy and went straight to Naples. Man, when Castro heard about it, he went crazy. To teach him a lesson, he had Pedro towed out, and it was far, man, in a little shit-assed dinghy. He kept him out there, with no water or food, for like, a day and a half."

"Guy could've died."

"He said the only way to make sure nobody opened their mouths was to set examples. It worked, you know, but people, they like to talk."

"Did Julio Castro arrange for Gustavo Flores, the shooter at the trailer, to ambush us?"

He nodded.

"He asked you to set it up?"

"He told me to make it just a scare, that he never wanted to rile you guys up. I said it was a bad idea, but you can't say no to Castro."

"So you're saying that Flores went rogue?"

"I don't know what happened."

Jackson was lying. He was trying to distance his culpability in the attack.

"If Flores didn't follow orders, what would have happened?"

"It didn't matter, man. Gustavo was dead before he got to the trailer. The boss wouldn't even give him the chance to link back to him with something like that."

To me, we had enough to pin conspiracy to murder on Castro. Maybe we couldn't pin the ambush on him in court, but that was okay. We knew it was him, and he was going away for a long time.

It was time for action.

45

———

THE CHEROKEE'S TIRES SCREECHED AS I PULLED INTO A SPOT. I was going to be a couple of minutes late for the meeting with the sheriff and the head of prosecution. Mary Ann had been throwing up all night, and now I wouldn't get there before the prosecutor did.

One of my rules in a meeting with more than two people was to get in the room first or second. That way, I believed that anyone after me was coming into my space. It was an advantage in my eyes. It may have been an illusion, but it made me feel better. It was especially important when the others came from a similar background.

Flinging the door to the stairwell open, I kept thinking that Chester and David Bromley were cut from the same cloth. The sheriff wasn't a lawyer but a politician and looked for the worst-case scenarios. It was exactly what attorneys were programmed to do.

I didn't want them to buddy up, making a team if an objection came up. But when I saw the two of them talking in a hushed tone over a cup of coffee, that hope went out the window.

The sheriff had his jacket off, but Bromley was in his funeral-director suit. Chester motioned to an empty chair.

"Would you like a cup of coffee, Frank?"

"I'm fine, sir."

I exchanged greetings with Bromley, confirming he'd make a helluva undertaker.

Chester said, "Let's get this going. My schedule is chockablock today. Now, I read the Jackson briefing, why don't you give the both of us some color on where we stand with the case?"

"Terry Jackson was as close a confidant that Julio Castro had. He's confirmed that Castro ordered the attack on Detective Dickson and killed several others, including the informant we were going to meet. He also instructed him to assassinate Arturo Lopez, who was the first to help us identify Castro as the leader of the drug ring."

Chester said, "Exactly how does he know this?"

I explained that Castro told Jackson what to do and that he farmed it out to others.

Chester said, "How do you think he'll hold up on the stand?"

"He's tough and knows that if he doesn't come clean, our deal is off."

Bromley said, "What I'm concerned about it is his credibility."

"He's credible. This guy worked closely with Castro."

"I understand that, Detective, but he was part of the conspiracy to murder. He instructed others to carry out the order to kill. A defense attorney will pick him apart."

"But we've given him immunity."

"Precisely my point. The defense will argue that his motivation is to blame Castro for everything in exchange for his freedom."

Chester said, "Castro's defense team, and, with his money, I'm sure he'll get the best, will only need to convince a single juror that the testimony is tainted."

"What proof do you have that Jackson was close to Castro? Have you observed them together? Are there photos of the two of them?"

"No."

"That's unfortunate. The defense will argue that he's inflating his importance. They'll say that you've conducted weeks of twenty-four-by-seven surveillance and yet have no proof the men even know each other."

Chester said, "That's a good point."

"We can place them at the same location—"

"That's not the standard. Do you have another witness who can corroborate the relationship?"

"We also obtained information from Arturo Lopez, another member of the gang."

"Excellent. That's exactly what we need. And he's willing to testify?"

"He can't. Lopez was executed. Castro gave the order after he talked with us."

"That's unfortunate. Is there anyone else?"

"Not at the moment."

"I'd suggest you work on that. Otherwise, it amounts to hearsay. I'm not even sure a judge would allow the testimony, given Mr. Jackson is receiving immunity as a result."

"But he's close to Castro; he handles all the cash for him."

"That may be the case; however, where's the evidence beyond what one man, whose character is suspect, said?"

"Hold on. We've had eyes on the gang; we know what they're up to. The fact is, these bastards ambushed us."

"Detective, surely you know there's a major difference between a fact and one that can be proven to a jury."

Chester said, "We'll get them. But at this point, it seems David has concerns over whether this is winnable. You need to do some additional work here: develop concrete, prosecutable evidence on Castro."

More work? What the hell did he think I'd been doing out there? "I can get what you need if you can get me a warrant to search both Castro's house and the Jasmine Street one."

"Do you see a judge signing off on this based upon what we have?"

"It's thinner than we'd like, but if it's constructed properly and we submit it to Judge Foster, we stand a good chance at approval."

Resolved is how I left the meeting—resolved to draft the subpoena request in a way to gain approval and resolved that I'd be leaving the department eventually. There was no way I could continue working here. All I wanted was a bit of support, and Chester just couldn't deliver.

Even the previous crusty old sheriff, who despised anyone who wasn't born in the county, had more tact when meeting people outside the department. He and his predecessors never took sides. If they had something to say, they said it in private. It was the only way to earn the loyalty and respect of those putting themselves in harm's way.

I labored much longer than usual drafting the request. Initially, each draft sounded good until I read it back. It took me two hours to finalize it, and, just before heading upstairs with it, I reread it.

Tearing it into pieces, I started from scratch, sticking to the facts and striking my instincts and emotions when they appeared on the page. It took me another hour, but I was feeling good about it.

Before delivering it, I called Bilotti and read it to him. He was neither cop nor lawyer, but the doctor was the smartest guy I knew. After hanging up, I made the change he suggested and headed upstairs.

46

———————

Word was that the warrant request was sitting on Judge Foster's desk. It had been almost two days since I submitted it. The seeds of doubt were being watered with every passing hour.

Watching Castro's house, where nothing was happening, didn't make the wait any easier. Judge Foster's clerk was a gal I'd dated when I first moved down from Jersey.

It was through pure luck that I hadn't burned the bridge with her, something I was prone to do after my divorce. The gal's mother in Minnesota had taken ill, and she took a leave of absence to care for her. By the time she came back, I had gone through cancer surgery and started dating my former partner, Mary Ann.

I made an internal call to the old flame. After the pleasantries, I asked her if she knew if the judge had signed the warrant. She said he was presiding over a trial where the defense was filing a relentless onslaught of motions. She said today's session was going to be adjourned at one and he should review it then.

Thanking her, I saw Castro's garage door rise. I rushed her off the phone and leaned toward the screen. It looked like him getting into his Mercedes SUV.

As he pulled out of the garage, I zoomed the video in. Castro was behind the wheel. I followed him as he drove out of Park Shore and onto Route 41. When he took Pine Ridge Road to Airport Pulling Road, I wondered if Castro was taking a heavily trafficked route to prevent being tailed.

He kept heading south. Was he going to Everglades City? He crossed over Golden Gate Parkway and my stomach turned. Naples Airport, a bastion of private jets, was just ahead.

I stood as he turned right onto Radio Road. Castro was going to the airport. The fact he didn't seem to have bags had me hoping he was picking someone up.

He parked and got out. Castro didn't open the trunk, instead, he walked past the rental car area, heading toward a silver jet sitting outside a hangar.

Where was he going? I couldn't track him if he was flying. The stairs were down on the silver plane. Castro grabbed the handrail and was inside the cabin in a flash. The stairway retracted, and the jet taxied toward the runway.

I grabbed the phone. "Connolly, Castro is about to take off out of Naples Airport. Is there any way we can track him?"

"Not with the drones."

"We'll have to grab the flight plans."

"That's if they file any."

"They better have. I got the tail number and will call the tower. Let me know if you see anything happening in Everglades. I'm getting the feeling somebody tipped him off."

"It could be nothing. He could be visiting someone."

"He had no bags."

"Oh boy. Well, maybe it's just a day trip or something."

"My gut's telling me he's running. Keep your eyes open."

It took a bit of arm twisting, but I found out where the jet was heading. I fell back into my chair. It was destined for the Cayman Islands. Even more depressing was that the single passenger on board was listed as a man named Joseph Smith.

I cursed Chester and Bromley. The two of them let Castro slip through our hands. At this point, it'd take an extended legal battle, one that could last years, to extradite him to the United States.

Even worse, there was no guarantee that he wouldn't slip out of Cayman or that we'd get a federal judge to sign an extradition order. I was screwed. I'd never get revenge for Derrick.

I called back Connolly and told him what I learned. He was as bummed as me. I asked him to watch the feed from Castro's house. I needed to clear my head before informing Chester.

Before I got out of my chair the phone rang. It was the sheriff.

"I had to twist his arm a bit, but Judge Foster just signed off on the warrants."

That was bullshit. He'd never pressure a judge, nor would anyone wearing a black robe allow themselves to be bullied. "Unfortunately, it's too late."

"What are you talking about?"

"Castro just left on a private jet that's on its way to the Cayman Islands."

"Uhm. Well, I think you should execute the searches, obtain the additional evidence you need, and we'll drag him back to the States."

"I was just coming to see you about this. Are you free?"

"Give me ten minutes."

STEPPING OUTSIDE THE BUILDING, I put my sunglasses on. The warmth felt good. The air-conditioning was too cold for me and half of the people working inside. The problem was that the other half felt the place was too warm.

A hundred yards away was a set of park benches. All but one was shaded by oak trees. I parked my ass on the one in the sun and raised my face toward the vitamin D factory, hoping for a mood change.

Coincidences and me were not the closest of friends. I was always uncomfortable when someone explained away a happening as pure chance. To me it was possible evidence. What was behind Castro's departure to a place outside the immediate reach of US law enforcement?

Had the trip been planned? If so, why use an alias? Was he visiting his money, possibly arranging to transfer some to another private haven? I forced myself to think of it that way.

The alternative was a leak in the sheriff's office. A dirty cop who was feeding Castro information. It was much rarer than Hollywood liked to portray, but I couldn't discount the possibility.

I ran through the people who knew of the operation. Connolly and Brendan White knew the most, but both were solid cops. A mental check didn't come up with any questions either of them asked that in hindsight could be viewed as troublesome.

Moving on, I sifted through the men and women on the fringes. The only place I couldn't nail everyone down on was staging Jackson's death on Capri Island. No one knew who Jackson was, I reasoned.

I moved to another bench out of the sun. The idea that Jackson had double-crossed me popped into my thoughts. I called one of the two cops guarding Jackson at the safe house. They confirmed he hadn't made any calls.

It was time to talk this over with Chester. I had a thought and wanted to handle things my way.

47

I STOPPED BY THE OFFICE TO GRAB MY SPORTS JACKET. SURE enough, sitting in my in-box was an envelope containing the warrants. One damn day earlier, and everything would look different. Some would call it following the law, but I shoved it right into the bureaucracy column.

Walking up the stairs, I told myself it was another reason the time to retire had come. We had Castro in our sights and he had slipped away. We had a chance to get justice for Derrick plus put an evil drug gang out of business, but the system blew it.

Smiling at Chester's secretary, I feigned interest in an issue of *Police Chief Magazine* sitting on a side table. I had to avoid getting a whiff of her heavy perfume. Her husband must have olfactory issues; there was no way you could get used to such a musty smell.

Chester was on the phone. I heard him say goodbye, and a second later he told me to come in.

He took his readers off and said, "I guess we obtained the authority later than needed."

I wanted to say damn right it was. But I opted for, "It's

unfortunate, but there's always the possibility that someone tipped Castro off."

"That's the second time you've insinuated that we have a leak in the department. If you have something, now is the time to reveal it."

"I'm only raising the possibility, sir. I'll admit the thought may have come out of frustration."

"That's understandable. Let's go see what we can get out of these locations to build a case. It'll take time, but we'll drag him back to face justice."

To him, it was a case that would be handed over to the feds. It would be off his desk, and Chester wouldn't be the one to tell Derrick that it might be a couple of years, if at all, before Castro would pay for what he did.

"The two extraditions I've been involved with took years."

"The sooner we get the evidence we need, the quicker we can get the State Department involved."

"We should wait a couple of days before executing the warrants."

"I totally disagree. If Castro is onto us, he'll alert his minions, and any evidence that exists will be at risk of being destroyed. Then we'd have nothing."

"With all due respect, sir, we have nothing now. What we have is the hope that after a year or more some bureaucrat is going to understand the gravity of our case. It's possible, but I doubt it. Even if the State Department does its part, how likely do you think some slob in the Caribbean is going to do the right thing? Especially with the kind of money Castro has stashed."

"You can't control everything. We do our part; that's all we can do. What happens after that is out of our jurisdiction. I want the warrants executed, now."

An idea I thought could work came to mind. "Hear me out a second, sir. The possibility that Castro was spooked into leaving is a real one."

"Are you back to insinuating we have a leak in the department?"

"I'm not saying he was tipped off, though it's possible, but he could have gotten info on our surveillance. Maybe someone saw the refueling at the airport. I think it's worth a shot cracking down on Platt. We shut down the marijuana pipeline, and Castro would think Platt was the target. Plus, it'd be a nice moment for the department."

Chester suppressed a smile. "That's an interesting theory."

Time to feed his ego. "We'd have to make a big deal about it. Get lots of media coverage to make sure it gives us the camouflage we need to make Castro feel safe enough to come back."

"The idea is growing on me."

The media images of a large seizure of weed had Chester mesmerized, not the idea of fooling Castro into returning.

"We're going to have to bring Platt down anyway. Who knows, we might get lucky."

"If we do this, I want it done immediately."

"Of course. It would be more effective that way."

"How long would you want to wait after arresting Platt?"

"I'd say a week. Just to be sure."

"That's too long. I'll agree to three days after you shut down the marijuana smugglers. In the meantime, prepare your search teams. I want everything ready to go."

THE NEXT DAY we grabbed Platt and two others at his Plantation Island home, along with sixty-two pounds of marijuana. The blocks of pot made great shots. And the media ran with it. Stories about the revival of the weed pipeline dominated the news for two days.

Chester sucked up the spotlight, but I made sure to do a TV interview on *WINK News* in case anyone had seen me in Everglades City. It was a win for me and the department, but I didn't feel good. Chester's deadline of three days was rapidly approaching.

With all the attention the sheriff was basking in, I knew I could squeeze a day or two more out of him. But I was also aware that time was running out.

48

————

LYING IN BED, I BEGAN READING THE DA VINCI BOOK. IT WAS surprising to learn he was a vegetarian. I considered the possibility he was the world's first one, and the next thing I knew my cell was ringing. Reaching over to the nightstand, I saw the thick tome on the floor. I'd fallen asleep reading. Again.

"Hello?"

"Frank, you're not gonna believe it, but guess who just drove up Castro's driveway?"

The guessing nature of the question made me think of Derrick. "Prince Charles."

"None other than Castro himself."

"Are you sure?"

"A hundred percent. After he pulled the Mercedes in the garage he opened the trunk. There's no doubt it's him. He's back. What do you want to do?"

As much as I'd thought about it, I hesitated. It wasn't wise to share information sooner than necessary. Connolly had integrity, but he was also human. "Just keep your eyes on him. I have a couple of things I need to organize."

"That's it?"

"And don't forget to watch the house on Jasmine. Let me know if there's any activity at either place."

"You got it. Talk to you later."

"Hold on. I need you to keep quiet about this. I don't want anybody to know he's back. Nobody on the force, not your wife, your brother, nobody. Is that clear?"

"Sure, Frank. I don't tell anybody anything."

"Good, keep it that way. Make sure you drink enough coffee to stay awake. I'm coming in."

Mary Ann put her Kindle down. "You're going to the office?"

I headed to the closet. "I have to, Castro came back. I gotta say, I'm stunned. I mean, I was hoping he would, but after two days went by, I figured we lost him."

"You're going to raid the houses tonight?"

I strapped my shoulder holster on. "Not tonight. I want to line everything up. We'll probably hit them in the early morning at the same time."

"I don't want you going in. You can manage it, but that's it."

I held my bulletproof vest. "I'll be okay, don't worry."

"No, Frank. I mean it. We can't take chances. This gang is dangerous; they don't respect the cops or anything."

"It's going to be all right."

"That vest isn't magic, you know. It didn't prevent Derrick from getting hurt."

"Don't you think I know that? I live with that goddamn fact every day."

"Take it easy, Frank. I just don't want you putting yourself, and this family, at risk trying to get revenge."

Even though I always gave her the BS about justice, she knew I was motivated by revenge. It brought to mind one of my favorite quotes: "The best revenge is one that goes too far." "I'll be okay."

"Promise me you'll stay out of danger."

"Don't worry, we're just going to execute the search warrants. We'll have plenty of support, and like I said, we'll do it while they're still in bed."

I kissed her cheek. "I'll see you tomorrow, sometime after lunch."

As soon as I got in the Cherokee, I called Cisco. He quickly agreed to come in and set the raid up. My appreciation quickly melted into concern.

I considered him one of the most dependable people in the department, but Cisco seemed a little too eager to come in instead of going to bed. Was there a chance he wanted to be there to tip off Castro?

AT NIGHT, the station had a different personality. There were fewer people around, but there was more electricity. Collier County had fewer crimes than most towns, but the majority of arrests happened at night.

On the way to see Cisco, I passed the fingerprinting room. Someone was getting inked. Booking someone took a lot of time and paperwork. It ensured a steady stream of activity, even on the slowest of evenings.

Exiting the second-floor stairwell, the mood changed. The administrative and sheriff's offices were skeletally staffed on the overnight shift.

Cisco shared an office with Lieutenant George Riordan, who ran the county's property and evidence bureau. Cisco wasn't behind his desk, but Riordan was. What was he doing here this late?

"Hi George, how's it going?"

"Not bad. How about you?"

"Good. Isn't it past your bedtime?"

"We're moving into the new evidence room they built. Chester's boy wants it done overnight. God forbid we disturb anybody during regular hours."

"I forgot about that. It's bigger?"

"Oh yeah. Almost twice what we have now."

Cisco walked in with a cup of coffee. "Hey, Frank. You want to grab a cup?"

"Nah, had one on the way here."

"Sit down."

"Thanks for coming in. You didn't seem to mind."

"My old lady was watching the Hallmark Channel; you did me a favor. So how we going to do this?"

I looked over at Riordan. Cops were trained to keep their eyes open but also to listen covertly. "Let's go see Connolly."

We walked a couple of doors down. It was ideal. The redhead was glued to a pair of monitors, and the desks around him were empty.

"Any activity?"

"Besides a couple of guys going out back to smoke at Jasmine, it's quiet."

"Have you established the time between cigarette breaks? Last thing we need is to be ready to pounce and somebody steps out for a nicotine fix."

"It varies. But that's a good point. We should go right after a smoke to avoid detection. We'll keep back, watch the drone feed, and then move in."

"Nah, I want both houses served at the same time."

Cisco said, "We'll need a dozen men, six for each place."

"That's too many. We'll stand out. These neighborhoods are quiet."

"That's what's needed. There are multiple males in the Jasmine Street home. We need to have the proper force if things go south."

"Granted. Get the six for Jasmine, but don't tell anyone where they are headed until they get to Everglades City. For the Devil's Lane location, I want a minimal presence. He's alone in the house."

"No less than four. Two guarding the exterior, someone to deliver the warrant, and a backup, twenty yards away. But I'd like a fifth."

"It'll be me and three others. We'll be fine, I'll tag him with the warrant and hand him off so we can search the premises."

"You sure about that?"

Though Mary Ann's warning resounded in my head, I said, "Absolutely."

49

I PUT MY PROTECTIVE VEST ON. BEFORE CLOSING THE DOOR to my locker, I touched the picture of Mary Ann pasted to the side. I started to leave but turned around and opened the locker.

Reaching into the back, I pulled out my old vest. I took the metal plate out of the chest sleeve and slipped it into the rear compartment of the one I had on.

Passing the firearm vault, I thought about grabbing a couple of assault weapons. We were going to execute search warrants; it wasn't a raid. Or was it? There was no doubt we'd find enough evidence to arrest Castro and his gang. The unknown was whether they were armed and, if so, how heavily.

We knew Julio Castro had a legal gun permit. In fact, he had three pistols that we knew of. He was a careful man but one who ordered the killing of his own men.

The so-called Professor might be brilliant, but he was also ruthless. Even so, I couldn't see him engaging us. He'd lose. Castro's way out of the mess I was creating for him was either with expensive lawyers or to run.

Given the way he used a private jet and an alias to fly to the Cayman Islands, there was a good chance he'd try to arrange another clandestine flight out. I'd have to make sure the recent trip was something a judge knew about if we ended up arresting him.

We didn't have enough intel on the men in the Jasmine Street house. The prudent thing to do was to go with an overwhelming force. The picture of Derrick lying in a pool of blood flashed through my mind.

I stuck my head down the next aisle of lockers. "Listen up, I want each of you to take an assault rifle along."

As they filed to the cabinet, I went to my office. We were leaving in ten minutes. It was safe to send the inquiry on who was behind the Cayman Islands' shell companies.

WITH CONNOLLY in the passenger seat, and Officers Gomez and Fuentes in the rear, I turned onto Neapolitan Way in the dark. We pulled into the Publix parking lot and waited. It was 5 a.m. The team heading to Everglades City had left fifteen minutes before us.

"Coty just texted. They're approaching the Route Twenty-Nine intersection."

"Tell him to let us know when they get to the overpass."

Five minutes later, Connolly said, "They're in the city."

It was 5:08. When the clock turned to 5:10, I put the car in drive. "Let's get going."

Turning back onto Neapolitan Way, I drove west, passing Devils Lane. I made a right onto Crayton Road and another one on Parkwood Lane. At the intersection of Devil's Lane, I slowed down.

"Castro's house is in the row of houses behind these. See if you can pick anything out."

I turned onto the street. A white car was backing out of a driveway at the far end of the street by Castro's home. It was coming in our direction.

"Shit. Get down, out of sight."

The first thing I noticed was the sticker on the windshield. It was for MBA, the taxi service that made airport runs. Was Castro on the run? As it passed, I held my breath and peered in the back seat.

"It's clear. It was a taxi with a woman."

Then I started bouncing around the possibility that he was using a disguise as I made a U-turn. It was 5:16.

"Tell them I want the warrant served at five thirty-five sharp."

"Done."

I parked in the cul-de-sac at the end of Devil's Blight. In between two houses, I caught a glimpse of Venetian Bay. The water was dark and calm. We went over our positions, and when the clock hit five thirty, I said, "It's showtime," and drove out of the block.

I cut the engine, and before rolling to a stop, Connolly said, "They served the Jasmine warrant. They got three suspects under arrest."

"What? They went in?"

"Looks that way."

"They jumped the damn gun." I opened the door. "Let's get going. Turn your body cams on."

I jumped at the pssting sound of the sprinklers starting up. Eyes on the door as I crossed the lawn, the shade over the right-hand window fluttered.

I reflexively drew my pistol and stood off to the side of the door, giving the officers time to get to the rear of the home. Extending my arm, I rang the bell three times, then rapped the door with my fist.

"Answer the door, you bastard," I muttered.

Stepping in front of the door, I pressed the bell half a dozen times and pounded on the door.

"Police. Open the door. We know you're in there, Castro."

I let two minutes go by and turned to Connolly. "Get the Halligan bar."

Hurricane codes mandated that exterior doors in Florida open out. The battering rams we used up north wouldn't work.

I took the crowbar-like device and wedged it between the door and frame. On the second attempt, the wood splintered. "You circle to the left."

Hugging the wall, I shouted, "Julio Castro, this is the police. Come out with your hands up."

The only sound was the hum of the air-conditioning. Sticking my gun into the kitchen, I tucked my chin down and stepped in. Nothing but the sleekest kitchen I'd ever seen.

"Connolly, you good?"

"Yeah. Cleared two bedrooms."

Castro had to be in the house. The drone surveillance didn't show him leaving. I hoped like hell that Connolly hadn't fallen asleep when it was his turn to monitor the Devils Lane home.

Holding my pistol with both hands, I headed to a pair of double doors leading to the master bedroom suite. "Castro, this is the police! Stop playing games and come out."

An unmade bed with a headboard that spanned the entire wall anchored the powder-blue room. I bent down; he wasn't hiding under it. A hallway lined with his-and-her closets led to a white bathroom.

The lady's closet had three pieces of luggage and scores

of empty hangers. Castro's closet was filled with clothes and a floor-to-ceiling rack of footwear.

The shower area had a waist-high wall blocking the view. Creeping forward, I pictured Castro kneeling behind it. He wasn't. I looked around the door to the toilet area, noticing there was urine in the bowl.

"Frank?"

"In here."

"Where the hell is he?"

"You sure you kept him under twenty-four seven?"

"Absolutely."

"You didn't doze off?"

"No way."

"He's got to be in here somewhere. Let's check the attic."

Connolly pulled down the attic stairs from a hallway outside the guest bedrooms. A breeze of cool air streamed toward the opening as he climbed up. Connolly flicked on his flashlight before sticking his head into the heat.

I heard his footsteps and held my breath until he yelled, "It's all clear."

As he climbed down the stairs I wondered if the bastard had gotten away somehow. "Get Gomez and Fuentes in here."

Connelly left to get the officers guarding the home's perimeter. I went into the main room. It had a casual elegance to it. As opposed to the modest landscaping, the interior was top shelf.

Though I'd never been in one, it felt like a Manhattan loft. The walls were covered in large, textured paintings. The pieces were strong and drew me in. Castro was a cold-blooded killer with good taste.

I opened the drawer to a chest covered with ostrich skin and was sorting through it when my colleagues entered.

"Did either of you see anything outside?"

50

IN STEREO, THEY RESPONDED, "NO."

"You kept the sides of the house in view? At all times?"

"Yes, sir. I was on the left corner, with a sight line to the street, and Fuentes was on the other side."

"We didn't see him."

"Nothing suspicious? Anything, no matter how small?"

They shook their heads.

"Okay, let's give this place a going-over. Let's start in here."

A large rug made of short animal hair covered most of the family room. It had geometric patterns formed out of slight color variations in the hides. It was off-centered. A clear coffee table that looked like plastic anchored the middle of it.

It looked light enough, but I wasn't going to blow my back out.

"Help me move this."

After setting the Lucite furniture in a corner, we rolled up the carpet.

"Look what we have here."

"That's, like, the biggest one I've seen."

A door to a safe was set into the foundation. Its touch pad turned red when I tapped on it.

"Call the office. Tell them we need someone to crack this open."

My first thought was the safe would be filled with money. Maybe even drugs. Then it hit me that Castro could be hiding in the safe. But I quickly shot down the idea. There was no way he could have moved the table and rug back in place if he were below.

He had to be hiding somewhere else. I surveyed the room, going wall by wall. I walked to a row of stacked pieces of square paintings hanging near a pass-through. I knocked on the wall. It was solid.

"Keep your eyes open. Check the floors and walls for a hiding place. He's got to be in here somewhere."

Castro's office had enough wood to make him responsible for deforesting a couple of acres. Bookshelves lined one wall. It was the type of setting that Hollywood used for access to hidden rooms.

I pushed against each section. There was no give. Was there a releasing mechanism of some kind? I ran my hand beneath each shelf, failing to locate a button.

The room's floor had the grain of an exotic wood. I looked for a seam that would signal a doorway but came up empty. I studied the ceiling and its ornate molding before leaving the room.

Connolly said, "Cisco just called back. He said someone from Safe and Sound would be here within the hour."

"Good. By the way, are you sure you looked everywhere in the attic?"

"Yeah, why?"

"One time I caught a suspect hiding up there. He was nestled in by the air handler. I almost missed him."

"The whole place is sprayed with foam insulation. Unless he's disguised as a roof joist, he's not up there."

Just off the kitchen was a wet bar with a wall of wine behind glass doors. I opened a door and pulled out a bottle. It was a French Bordeaux. I reached for the tile wall behind the display and knocked my knuckle on it. I checked the grout lines. They were all solid. I slipped the bottle back on the rack and closed the door.

Wondering if Castro might be hiding behind the kitchen cabinetry, I started pulling pots and pans out and knocking on back panels.

Connolly said, "What are you doing?"

"Seeing if there's any false backings in here."

"It's a lot easier to check using a thermal sensor."

I pulled my head from under an electric stove top. "A what?"

"A thermal sensor. It detects hidden heat sources."

"Right. I read about them and those infrared readers. You have one?"

"I have an app on my phone."

He showed me how it worked, and I downloaded the app onto my phone. "You start in here. I'm going to start back in the master."

I went straight to the closets. I dumped Castro's clothes on the floor and ran the phone over the wall. The screen's color remained a shade of green that reminded me of the Gulf of Mexico. He wasn't behind these walls.

Next was the empty closet. I slid the phone along the back wall. Toward the center the color changed to orange. When I moved it toward the corner it turned red. I stepped back and stared at the wall. Could it be?

It was on an outside wall. I tried to find a spot where the

wall could hinge but the closet racking covered the corner. I left to get help.

Connolly and I were in the closet. Gomez and Fuentes stood behind us. Connolly swung a hammer at the Sheetrock. He pulled it out, taking a chunk of wallboard with him.

He repeated the process, using his hands to rip a large section of wall away. There was nothing but insulation behind it.

As Connolly peered into the hole he'd made, I said, "How can that be?"

"To the left there's a nice crack. Must be from settling. The outside air is getting in."

Where the hell was he? Between the urine in the bowl and the messy bed, he was in the house. The only possible thing was he somehow slipped out without our guys seeing him. *The Invisible Man* he wasn't.

I sent Gomez and Fuentes to scan temperatures in the guest bedrooms, and Connolly and I went to the kitchen. After we pulled out the fridge and came up empty, I opened the door to a large pantry.

It was well stocked. There was enough nonperishable food to last a couple of months. I shoved aside a shelf full of pasta boxes when the bell rang and a voice called out.

"Hello, hello! I'm from Safe and Sound. They said you needed a safe opened."

I turned to Connolly. "Go open the door for this guy and show him the safe."

The shelving to the right was all canned goods. I parted a section filled with more tuna fish than Publix offered. Nearing the wall, the color of my phone's screen changed from blue green to a mass of orange.

I pulled the phone away and the orange disappeared.

Slowly I eased the phone against the wall. The orange turned red. There was a heat source behind the wall.

Was it something mechanical generating the heat, or was Castro hiding in a compartment? Running my hand along the bottom of the last pullout, I didn't find anything.

The top shelf was crowded with paper towels and napkins. Reaching up, I stuck my hand in and probed the corner. There was something there. I stood on my toes and detected a metal latch.

Quietly, I grabbed a kitchen chair and took a look. A stainless-steel U-shaped pull was connected to a cable. Was this the access trigger?

51

———

THE CABLE SNAKED ALONG THE BACK PART OF THE SHELVING. I tugged the lever, and the pullouts rolled into my gut. I released the cable and shoved them back into place.

I bent down to put the chair back and noticed a button on the lower inside of the doorjamb. It was smaller than an M&M. I pushed it. A loud click sounded. The left-handed bank of shelving pulled away from the wall.

I drew my weapon. My heart pounded like a parade drum. With the muzzle of my pistol, I pried the cabinetry open. The three-by-four-foot space was lit by an LED high hat. Seated on an upholstered bench was Julio Castro. Lying next to his right thigh was a 9mm Glock.

My gun was pointed at his head. Though I wanted to put a bullet between his beady eyes, I eased the pressure my finger had on the trigger.

"Put your hands up!"

His hand slid off his lap. Toward the pistol. My mind went blank. I squeezed the trigger.

Bang!

52

______

DROPLETS OF BLOOD SPRAYED ME. THEY SEEMED TO BE moving in slow motion. The blood hit my vest. Castro's head banged off the wall. Ears ringing and gun pointed, I watched his head loll forward.

The muffled sound of people yelling pushed me to grab Castro's weapon. I clicked the safety on and stuck it in my pants. Reaching for his neck, I checked for a pulse. Connolly, Fuentes, and Gomez rushed in.

Castro was gone.

"Holy shit! You got him."

"He, he was reaching for his gun, I had to shoot him. There was no choice."

"Serves the bastard right. The mother jumper shot Derrick."

"You got him right between his frigging eyes."

"Shit, look at this place. He's got enough stuff in here to hide for months."

Stepping into the kitchen, I leaned against the counter. My heart slowed to a drum roll. Holding my gun out to Connolly, I said, "Hold on to this until IA shows up."

He took it, and I turned Castro's over as well. I pulled my phone out. "Don't touch nothing. I got to call this in."

"No, man, I'll make the call. You take it easy."

"No, I have to do it."

I stepped outside. The kid from Safe and Sound was sitting in his van. He took a phone away from his ear as I approached.

"Everything is okay. I'm going to need you to hang around. After the suspect is removed from the premises, you can go back in and pop the safe open."

His face whitened. "He's dead?"

I nodded and walked away.

My hands shook as I dialed the office. I focused on what I needed to do, straining to hold a rush of rampaging emotions at bay. After reporting what happened, I asked to be transferred to the sheriff.

"Sir, I wanted you to know we got Castro."

"Well done, Frank. Everything go all right?"

"Not exactly. He was hiding with a Glock next to him. I told him to stand down, but he reached for it and—"

"You killed him?"

"I had no choice, sir. He was reaching for his weapon."

"Jesus Christ, Luca! What are you? A damn cowboy?"

"He was armed—"

"I heard that one before."

"But—"

"Now there's going to be another investigation and right after I overruled them for you. The timing couldn't be worse. You better be prepared."

I almost told him that I had my body cam on and did nothing wrong. Instead, I said, "I understand. I handed my firearm over to Connolly. Will you be calling IA?"

"Yes, is there anything else?"

"I know I have to be debriefed, but I'd like to stick around. We uncovered a safe buried in the slab, and the locksmith is waiting to open it."

"You know I can't allow that."

I wasn't surprised by the denial.

After hanging up, I punched in another number, starting the conversation the way he'd done a thousand times,

"Hey buddy, guess who we got today?"

Derrick said, "Castro? You nailed him?"

"Damn right I did." I lowered my voice. "Shot the bastard right between the eyes. We got the son of a bitch. He paid for what he did to you."

"How'd it go down?"

I gave him a summary and told him I'd call later. There was one more call I had to make before people started arriving at the scene. As the phone rang, I sat on the steps.

"Mary Ann . . ."

"Frank, are you all right?"

I exhaled. "I think so. We got Castro, but I-I-I had to kill him."

"Oh my God. Are you sure you're okay? Did you get hurt or anything?"

"I'm okay, just shaken up a little."

"Come home, Frank. Please, you need to rest."

"I can't yet. Let me get through with IA first."

An ambulance rolled up but what was needed was a body bag.

"You were out all night. You'll have a breakdown if you're not careful."

"I'm okay, really." A black sedan turned onto Devils Lane. "I got to go; Lacey just arrived."

EXCEPT FOR A LAMP in the family room, the house was dark. It was eleven thirty. I'd been going for a day and a half. The adrenaline had kept me going, but as I entered the bedroom, a wave of exhaustion hit me.

Mary Ann sat up. "I'm so glad you're home."

"Me too." I hugged her and felt my eyes well up.

"Everything go all right with IA?"

"Yeah, Lacey wasn't as big a jerk as usual."

"He probably saw the news. You're a hero."

"I saw some of it at the station. We'll see how long that lasts."

Between Derrick's heart-tugging interview on *WINK News* and FOX 4's coverage featuring a father who lost a daughter to drugs, I was the new savior.

"Jessica wanted to stay up to see you. When she first saw the news, she was very excited, but she really got scared when they said how dangerous it was."

"It wasn't too bad. I'll explain it to her in the morning. Make sure I see her before she goes to school."

"I'm going to keep her home tomorrow. We all need to be together."

I almost said no, but she was right. "Good."

"Come to bed."

Piling my clothes on the floor, I crawled into bed. Mary Ann shifted over and put her head on my chest.

"I'm so happy you're okay."

"It was bizarre. He was hiding in a room behind the pantry."

I felt wetness on my chest. "You could have . . . been killed."

"It's all over now."

"Go to sleep."

I lay there, exhausted but unable to sleep. I felt a sense of contentment over evening the score, but images of Castro sitting in the secret room kept invading my head. It forced me to examine whether I had to kill him or not.

After playing ping-pong with the possibility I'd acted too forcefully, I accepted the idea that I was right to feel good about killing him. The press seemed to agree, but I knew as more details emerged that I could go from hero to goat with the next newscast.

A wild card was Castro's culpability in the ambush. I believed he was, but we needed proof.

It might have been because it was the second life I'd taken, but Castro lying in the morgue didn't bother me like the first one had. It was a different feeling. It could have been the satisfaction that came with catching someone after a long chase, but I felt proud, satiated.

Even Lacey's questioning didn't upset me. Maybe it was my mindset or the support of the press, but Lacey and his IA minions hadn't rattled me.

They insinuated that I'd shot him out of revenge. They were right. The body cam hadn't shown much more than a finger tremor, but the Glock was in full view and my warning was clear.

Aside from wanting the evidence that Castro ordered the ambush, I didn't give a crap about anything else. Castro was dead, and I'd brought down his drug-dealing gang.

53

THE CALL FROM THE SHERIFF WAS THE BIGGEST SURPRISE since a new bike for my tenth birthday. He'd seen the body-cam video and felt I had been at risk. He never said it justified taking Castro's life, but that was Chester hedging.

His request to have me back working was almost as stunning. He gave me the bullshit that I knew the case, but it was because he had no one else. Connolly was good, but he was inexperienced and had come late to the investigation.

Though I wanted to tie up what may be my last case, I couldn't allow myself to say yes immediately. I called him just before five and said I'd be in the next morning.

I WAS at my desk before eight. Coffee in hand, I read the report detailing the search of Castro's house. The interior of the safe was four feet square, the largest I'd ever heard of. I picked up a photo. Six million in cash looked smaller than I'd expected.

Castro's two other guns had been in the safe, but neither

had recently been fired. There were no traces of drugs in the house. It didn't surprise me. Castro was too careful to be holding.

The safe also contained the deeds to three pieces of property on Grand Cayman Island. The dates of the purchases confirmed the reason for Castro's trip. It was a relief that we didn't have a leak in the department. Thinking the phrase, "Timing is everything" prophetic, I reached for the next document.

The printout of the Cayman Island inquiry made me smile. Julio Castro was the agent of record for the Blue Water Group, the company that owned the outfits that held the Jasmine Street house. There was no doubt Castro was connected to the drug ring.

Moving on, I read about evidence taken from the Jasmine Street home. It was a puzzle that an eight-year-old could piece together. The total amount of illicit drugs seized was just under three hundred grams.

We also took two scales that could measure to the hundredth of a gram, two cases of glassine envelopes, a stamp for the letter *C*, and enough stainless-steel tools to outfit an operating room.

What interested me and was certain to get the attention of the customs and border patrol and postal authorities were the courier- and priority-mail envelopes.

We had proof they were using the parcel companies to move drugs around. There were four shipments of fentanyl that were further disguised. The sender was a third-party seller on eBay. The cyber unit confirmed the Chinese shipper had a legitimate storefront selling sewing articles and patterns.

I had to admit, it was a smart way to use the system. What concerned me was how many others were using the supply chain to move drugs. It was a growing problem that was difficult to police. If some kind of technology wasn't deployed, we'd always be a step behind.

Taken into custody were two men: Miquel Garcia and Enrique Cepeda. Both had records. Even though their next conviction would subject them to three-strike sentencing, and with Castro dead, they weren't talking.

It was a twisted code many hardened criminals seemed to abide by. It was especially ironic, given that the guy they'd worked for was behind the deaths of their associates.

There was no doubt the world would be better off with these punks behind bars for decades. But I needed a witness to make sure Castro was a killer not just a drug lord. I didn't care which one we offered a deal to.

I needed intel on the men and made a call.

TERRY JACKSON WAS SQUIRRELED AWAY in an apartment across the street from Lowdermilk Park. The white two-story building was one of a block-long complex built in the sixties. It must have been a safe place because even I didn't know about it.

I texted the code for access and stood in the parking lot for them to verify me. A nod from a woman on a second-floor stairwell set me in motion.

Jackson was playing solitaire on a coffee table. He looked a couple of pounds lighter.

"How are you doing?"

"A lot better since Castro is dead."

"Amen. Look, we picked up two of his men from the Jasmine Street house: Miquel Garcia and Enrique Cepeda. What do you know about them?"

"They were around before me. Not the sharpest knives in the drawer, but they didn't step out of line and did a good job cutting and moving product."

"I need background on them. They kill anyone? Do they have any family? Is there anything I could use that would turn one of them against Castro?"

"You mean like Castro was screwing them with money or something?"

"Anything."

"He was pretty good with the guys. Everybody got what he promised them, and a lot of times Castro would give out bonuses. He didn't play favorites."

"Did they have to execute anyone?"

"Not that I knew of, but like I said before, Castro would order a hit, and there were a couple of levels to hide who had to do it. Guys would talk, you know, but I don't think they did any for him."

"Was there anyone he whacked that upset either of them?"

"If there was, they wouldn't say anything. The boss didn't like pushback."

"What about family?"

"They aren't married. Almost nobody is married in the gang."

"How about relatives in El Salvador?"

Jackson shook his head. "You know, Garcia's whole family was wiped out by La 18."

"They killed his entire family?"

"Yeah, that's why he hooked up with MS-13. They got him some revenge, but he still hates those guys."

I wondered how to use that information to get Garcia to turn.

"Do you know if Castro had any ties with La 18 or any gang other than MS-13?"

"Not that I know of."

"Let's say if he was working with La 18, you think knowing that would get Garcia to talk?"

"I guess so."

That was something I was going to consider fabricating. It could be what I was looking for.

"What about Cepeda?"

"He's really quiet. The only time I saw him get nuts was when one of the guys told a joke about some retarded kid. He got all pissed off about it and threatened him. I mean, he was right, you know, but it came out of nowhere."

"Maybe he knows someone or has a kid of his own with a disability."

"I don't know, man. He don't say much."

"You can't think of anything about either of them that we could use as leverage?"

"I don't see it, man."

54

———————

THE VIDEO FEED COMING OUT OF BOTH INTERVIEW ROOMS WAS similar. The faces of both men were frozen in defiance, and arms were crossed over their chests.

It was a coin flip on who to talk to first. I had nothing concrete to work with. It always amazed me that an offer to reduce a charge or even a grant of immunity wasn't enough motivation.

If it were a lesser sentence being traded, the reluctance came from the fear they'd be killed while behind bars. With Castro dead, the threat was vastly reduced, but thugs were good at frightening people.

I rapped on the door and stepped into the room. Miquel Garcia didn't look in my direction. He had a closely shaved head with a zigzag pattern over his ears. He was ten pounds from scrawny. I hit the recording device.

"Mr. Garcia, I'm Detective Luca. I know you're refusing to talk, and that's your right. I'm not going to waste time, but before I get to the point, I need to inform you of your right to counsel. If you cannot afford a lawyer, the county will provide a lawyer for you at no charge. Do you want an attorney present?"

"No."

"I have the authority to cut a deal with you. All you have to do is provide information about Julio Castro."

"Stop wasting your breath."

"Castro is dead."

He shook his head.

"You don't believe me that Castro is off the field?"

"It's not just him, man. There's all kinds of guys that'll come after me."

"You mean like MS-13?"

He shrugged.

"You know what we found out about your boss? That he was playing both gangs."

"What are you talking about?"

"He worked with MS-13 and La 18."

"No way, man."

"It's true."

"That's bullshit."

"You believe what you want to. You'll have plenty of time to think about it in jail. Like they say, three strikes and you're out."

He shrugged, but concern flashed across his face.

"I'm going to talk to your buddy and offer him a deal. I don't care who I make the trade with. I only got one gift to give, and the first one to talk gets it."

"Whatever."

I headed for the door. "It's not whatever, my friend. You're going away for a long time."

Garcia didn't say anything. Either it would take another run at him or he was a piece of stone. I left him to think it over.

I'd seen more than my share of hardened criminals, but these Latin American gangs were a different breed. Maybe it was the horrendous environment they'd come up in, or maybe it was a culture thing.

I peeked in on Cepeda. He was cracking his knuckles. I knocked and swung the door open.

He didn't move his head, but his eyes sized me up as I slid into a chair. I turned the recording devices on, introduced myself, and went over his rights. Cepeda declined the offer of counsel. A mistrust of lawyers was shared by many on both sides of the crime battle.

"Here's what I'm after, Mr. Cepeda. You help me with information on Julio Castro, and we'll make sure you avoid spending the rest of your life behind bars."

He shook his head and I said, "Before you answer, I want you to know that I made the same offer to your buddy Garcia, and he's asked for an attorney to review it. He takes it, we don't need you."

"Bullshit, Miquel would never do that."

"He's got two strikes against him, just like you. Nothing like the prospect of twenty-five years in prison to change a mind."

"You're bluffing."

"You think so? He gets a chance at a new start, and you'll rot away in a sweaty cell."

"I don't give a shit what happens to me."

"He'll be living it up with the reward money he gets."

"Reward money? For what? You paying him to talk?"

"No, the county and a couple of citizens put up money to get the person who ambushed my partner."

"How much?"

"More than two hundred thousand dollars, and he can use it any way he wants. He'll probably blow it all."

He shrugged.

"You said you don't care what happens to you, but you could do good with the money. Like help someone who needs it, you know, someone sick or with a disability."

"The money could go anywhere?"

"Absolutely."

"Out of the country?"

"Wherever and to whomever you want."

"You think the lawyer could make it so that no one but a certain person gets the money?"

"Sure. They'll set up something called a trust, and the money can only be used to take care of that person or two or three people, for that matter."

"Get me a lawyer. I'll do it, but the money's got to be guaranteed. If something happens to me, he's still going to get it."

"Don't worry. We can work it out."

55

I CALLED MARY ANN AND TOLD HER TO TAKE JESSIE AND meet me at Bleu Provence for dinner. Removing the doubt about Castro's involvement in the ambush was cause for celebration.

We were shown to a nice table, and as soon as we were seated, Jessie whispered, "Wow, this is a nice restaurant. I love the blue colors."

Mary Ann said, "We had our first date here."

I picked up the wine menu. It was as thick as the da Vinci book. "They have the largest collection I've ever seen." I thumbed through it, making it look like I was trying to decide on something before flipping to the owner's page of recommendations.

"You in the mood for a Pinot?"

"Whatever you want, Frank."

"There's a nice one, but it's eighty bucks. Let's go with the Rhone, it's thirty-three."

"That's still a lot, Dad."

"I know, but we're celebrating."

After I ordered the wine and a Sprite for Jessie, Mary Ann said, "So, what happened today?"

"One of the guys we arrested at the Jasmine house in Everglades flipped. He gave us more than enough to confirm Castro ordered the ambush."

"Didn't you kill him, Dad?"

"Yes, I had to. He could have hurt me if I didn't."

"So why does it matter, then?"

"It's important to know that he was the one behind it. If it wasn't for one of the men who worked for him giving us proof, well, let's just say that it makes me feel better about what happened."

The wine came. The server poured some into my glass. I looked at its color and then took a deep sniff, à la Bilotti. Was that blackberry I was smelling? I took a sip, and after a five-count gave the thumbs-up.

We clinked glasses. I said, "Here's to cutting deals when you have to." I took a gulp and rolled it around my mouth.

Mary Ann said, "I'm surprised one of them talked. Gang members don't usually snitch."

"It's ironic. This guy, Enrique Cepeda, decided to talk because of the reward money."

"It's always money, isn't it?"

"But in this case, he wanted the money for his brother. It seems his brother is disabled, and Cepeda wanted to make sure he was taken care of."

Jessie said, "That was nice of him."

"Nobody is a hundred percent bad or good, for that matter."

"Getting philosophical?"

"Maybe it's the wine."

MARY ANN CONVINCED me to take a leave of absence. That way I'd have up to a year to make sure I was making the right call.

Having that much wiggle room usually created doubt about decisions I'd made. However, the bottom line was I couldn't draw a pension at this time because I wasn't fifty-five. Money aside, thank God for that.

I leaned the framed license on a bookshelf and sat behind my desk. Primarily because of the news coverage, word had gotten out that I had left the sheriff's office to become a private investigator.

Initially, I was wary of the attention, but the publicity had generated a dozen calls looking to hire me. All the cases were mundane affairs. Except one. I read the notes I had taken about it when the doorbell rang.

I opened the door: it was Derrick and Lynn.

"The first day and you're late?"

I kissed his wife. "I'll take it from here."

"What time should I get him?"

"Give us three hours."

She kissed Derrick, and I wheeled him into the den.

"You want anything?"

"No, I'm anxious to get started. Tell me about this case."

I sat down. "John Talbot, fifty-seven years old and well-to-do. He went on a business trip to Atlanta."

"What's he do?"

"Engineering consultant."

"Okay. What else?"

"His wife gets a call from him. He says he's at the airport and is going to catch a flight at seven, arriving in Fort Myers at nine. Said he'd be home before ten. But he never showed up, never called, just disappeared."

"We start with the airline. Did he ever board the flight?"

"I spoke with Delta. He took an earlier flight from Atlanta, landing at Fort Myers at six p.m."

"Why would he tell his wife something different?"

"And where is Mr. Talbot?"

"I like this one."

I shook my head. "This private eye thing looks like it's going to be good for us."

***

The next book in this series is, Where Are They. Find it in eBook & Paperback.

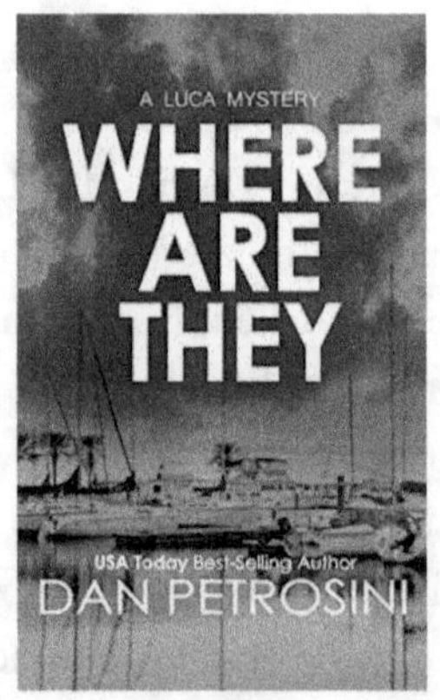

I hope you enjoyed reading this book as much as I enjoyed writing it. If you did, I'd appreciate it if you would write a quick review on Amazon or your favorite book site. Reviews are an author's best friend and even a quick line or two is helpful. Thanks, Dan

OTHER BOOKS BY DAN

Complicit Witness

Push Back

Ambition Cliff

You can keep abreast of my writing and have access to books that are free of discounting by joining my newsletter. It normally is out once a month and also contains notes on self- esteem, motivational pieces and wine articles.

It's free. See bottom of my website: www.danpetrosini.com

ABOUT THE AUTHOR

Dan is a USA Today and Amazon best-selling author who wrote his first story at the age of ten and enjoys telling a story or joke.

Dan gets his story ideas by exploring the question; What if?

In almost every situation he finds himself in, Dan explores what if this or that happened? What if this person died or did something unusual or illegal?

Dan's non-stop mind spin provides him with plenty of material to weave into interesting stories.

A fan of books and films that have twists and are difficult to predict, Dan crafts his stories to prevent readers from guessing correctly. He writes every day, forcing the words out when necessary and has written over twenty-five novels to date.

It's not a matter of wanting to write, Dan simply has to.

Dan passionately believes people can realize their dreams if they focus and act, and he encourages just that.

His favorite saying is – "The price of discipline is always less than the cost of regret"

Dan reminds people to get the negativity out of their lives. He believes it is contagious and advises people to steer clear of negative people. He knows having a true, positive mind set makes it feel like life is rigged in your favor. When he gets off base, he tells himself, 'You can't have a good day with a bad attitude.'

Married with two daughters and a needy Maltese, Dan lives in Southwest Florida. A New York native, Dan has taught at local colleges, writes novels, and plays tenor saxophone in several jazz bands. He also drinks way too much wine and never, ever takes himself too seriously.

He puts out a twice-a-month newsletter featuring articles, his writing and special deals and steals.

Sign up at www.danpetrosini.com